Angels & The Dark City of Trost

Book III of The Dark Angel Wars

Story and artwork

ISBN: 978-1-938743-14-6

This book is dedicated to my parents.

May you find peace and love in the afterlife.

I. The Champions

David sat at the long, oak table observing the interactions of those around him. There were subtle smiles, cold stares, and the nervous tapping of fingers against wood. His girlfriend's hand was rough, holding strong against the skin of his palm. She was keeping him grounded in reality, keeping him from idly entering the dimension of thoughts and dreams that belonged to others and merging them into reality. He and his friends were gifted beings from the land of Tahln, a once prosperous and beautiful land, now left dark and barren by the Shadow that had entered the land through the actions of his brother, Shekley.

Kialo, god of earth elements and king of Shea, sat at the end of the table. His skin was rough and burgundy with deep wrinkles carved into him like ravines. In contrast, his hair was white and wooly. A crown of antlers adorned with

2

ivy leaves, winter berries, and pinecones rested on his head. He wore long robes made of animal hides and fur which covered the length of his body. He held a wooden staff in his hand. His face was kind, yet fierce. To his right was an empty seat, a place that had been held for the sky goddess, who had refused any previous meetings about the subject matter at hand. She had expressed her distaste for what she called warmongering.

To his left sat Adrianna, the sea goddess. She had a mysterious gaze, one clouded and distant. Every time that David glanced at her, it was harder to read her and discern an emotion. At the moment, it was hard to make her out at all. She seemed hazy and translucent. Tendrils seemed to slowly curl and unfurl lazily every now and then, but David could not decipher their origin.

Beside her sat Amicus, the messenger god. He wore a simple brown robe, with a hood that shielded his face. He clutched a tall, wooden staff at his side. Across the table sat

friends and colleagues, friends that David knew well. All of

them were wearing the brown military clothes from their

own world. Among them was Sassy, one who took many

forms, but she sat now in her true form: a teenager with long

blonde hair which she had pulled into a tight ponytail. Her

honey-skinned face was still youthful despite the sadness in

her eyes. She sat with her knees up to her chest, chewing the

remains of gnawed fingernails. James was thin, his brown

hair was newly cut and he stared thoughtfully at the table

with his arms folded over his chest. Beside him was Kim, a

mahogany-skinned woman with long, black hair braided

down her back. She was responsible for the tapping fingers.

She sat with her chin resting in her hand and the other hand

tapped.

The gods were still holding out hope that the sky

goddess, Kristiniva, would fill the empty seat but they were close to starting without her again. The selbdes, the group of psychically gifted beings to which David belonged, were too nervous to speak out of order, and the gods seemed determined to stare into an oblivion while waiting for their queen.

Finally, Amicus stood. He turned to Kialo. "Father, I fear that we can wait no longer," he said, "for time is against us all."

The earth god nodded. "Perhaps she will come around soon," his voice sounded dull and disappointed. "Until then, our plans will proceed."

Amicus walked around the table and though his eyes were shielded, David could feel the god's stare aimed at him.

"We know what the Shadow is capable of." The messenger god's voice thundered strong, yet soft. "We have seen it in the memory of David. However, we need a new assessment to see if the Shadow's carrier, Shekley, has strengthened in power by traveling to Sark. We have called you here as volunteers to enter his stronghold, the misplaced city of Trost, and bring back information so that we can find his weakness and strike. We asked for volunteers to complete this task, and you are the ones who have taken it upon yourselves to complete this mission. You have the gratitude and favor of all the gods united here."

Amicus paused in his speech and stretched his hand toward the doors leading into the chamber. The elven guards opened the doors, and three creatures entered. The largest and most eye-catching was dark gray and black. It looked like a large, hairy rock with glittering ornaments and painted designs. It was hard to discern at first whether-or-not it was a male or female. It was towering and muscular, garbed in black fur. Shaggy, wiry, black hair fanned out around its head, almost like a mane. A large, round nose was in the middle of its face. Tusks protruded from its lower jaw and big, orange eyes stared down at the selbdes curiously. It was a rock troll.

The second largest was a tall, blue-haired sea elf with shining, silver-toned skin. He wore tall, gray, hide boots and a long, gray seafarer's coat. A matching hat adorned his head.

The third was hardly seen at all, except for the glowing light that flashed from above the elf's head. She was a light fairy. The three lingered in the doorway as Amicus announced them.

"These are the three chosen champions of Shea: Traegar, a rock troll from the Mountains of Yune, Aqualon, Prince of the Sea elves, and Iluma, a light fairy. There should be a fourth, but Kristiniva, goddess of the sky, has not chosen a champion. However, the three will give you great aid if you will take them." He waited for a response.

"Thank you," Shiana spoke, "we accept their help."

"A wise decision!" the sea goddess, Adriana exclaimed. Her voice hissed like sea spray.

"Bring forth your maps," Amicus said to David.

David nodded to Kim, who pulled a map from her pack and unrolled it on the table. They had been working long hours every day to create a map of Trost based entirely on memory. It had been drawn out on several pieces of scroll paper with a quill and ink pen. Each page was a layer of the city.

"How many layers did you say this city has?" Kialo asked.

"More than we know for sure," Kim responded. "These are the first few. None of us have ever had the opportunity nor the desire to go below the fifth level. It is rumored that there are mines in the lower levels, but as I said, none of us have ever been there. Hopefully, we will only need to worry about the top layer. The citadel itself is huge, and that is where Shekley will be. There is no doubt about that. He is almost always there. He lives there, he works there, and it is assumed that the Shadow will be there with him."

"This mission is to find Shekley, and see what his plans are. If there are any secrets to find they will almost certainly be in the citadel, under the control of the Shadow," David observed. "Anyone who goes in will undoubtedly have to face the Shadow and an army of Mahldrusecs."

Shiana turned her attention to the gods' champions. "This could be a fatal mission," she said to them. "We can do this, but I need reassurance that you understand the full extent of what you are volunteering for."

"I will fight to my death to save my people and serve my gods," Aqualon responded defensively. Traegar nodded

9

and made a grunting sound as she beat her fist on her chest. The faerie's light wavered and a musical sound emanated from the illumination that surrounded her.

"We understand and we have a desire to aid you," said Aqualon.

"Thank you," Shiana said. "We need all the help that we can get."

There had been long talks during and after the meeting. David had wanted to volunteer. He wanted to be the one to enter his brother's city, the one to finally bring an end to his brother's madness. He wanted his friends to stay in the safety of Shea, where the Shadow could not harm them, where they would not be hunted down and killed or tortured. David, however, would endanger everyone by entering the city. His gift was to bring illusions, and he was the cause of Shekley's madness. His illusions had driven Shekley away from him, from everyone. Shekley had been driven from madness to temptation, and finally to the Shadow: the essence of a dark god that had comforted him at first. It had promised him simple things. Success in school, the pretty girl he liked...but because Shekley's heart hardened and he could not resist the power of the Shadow's suggestions, he started wishing for darker things, sinister, insane things. His mind was no longer his own. Over time David had gone from listening and feeling innocent childhood wishes of a normal but misguided boy to the horror and confusion of a dark god's madness. He had been on that journey, often unwilling, into his brother's mind. The scarring would never leave his soul. The things he had witnessed, felt, experienced along with Shekley would forever haunt him. Now he was here, sending others to that darkness. The guilt was already welling inside of him.

Shiana squeezed his hand. "You are not sending us. We are going because we choose to. We are going to find a way to end his suffering as well as yours. We know the cost if we are caught. We understand the risk. Yet we still choose it."

David nodded. "Some part of me knows that, but my past gives me too many doubts".

"And mine gives me hope. I was working in that city for six months in an office, undetected, while I unraveled his plan to come here. I'm certain that we can go in now to figure out what the second part to his plan is."

"These other champions, though…they are not as easy to camouflage. They'll just be used in his experiments. Tortured. Killed..."

"They know the risk as well. They have gifts too, and despite all of the pacifist talk in this land, I can assure you that at least one of them has seen war before." David passed her a doubtful look.

"I'm serious. I've witnessed the memories of it in his mind. Aqualon, the sea elf. I've seen it. He knows so much more than he lets on."

"I should be the one going."

Shiana shook her head, red hair brushed against her shoulders. "But we need you here. You are the projectionist. You have to show the Sheans what I'm observing."

David knew that she was right. They each had a job. David would be projecting to the Sheans the things that Shiana sent him. She was the strongest telepath and could send images and speak to him over distances. Sassy could trick others into seeing her as anything she wanted them to. She could change her appearance at will. James would be going, as always, since he was one of the strongest healers.

Kim could see things before they happened, so she was usually ready to accept any mission.

Teri and Michael had not been in the meeting, but they volunteered to go. Teri's gift was to interpret languages of any race, including A.I. and computers. Michael was dangerous sometimes, as his gift was to cause immense explosions, but he usually went on missions. If no one else could defeat the mahldrusecs, he usually could. Explosions were useful in that way. However, this also usually ended in injury of some sort, since his explosions could not be controlled.

David went over lists in his mind of preparations that they would need to make. He was aware, from past experience, that no matter how prepared they were or would be, there was always some part of the equation that they couldn't see, something that no one could foresee.

Sometimes, those things could bring death for his friends, or sometimes it could bring great help, such as when they inadvertently ended up in Shea. They had been fed, clothed, and refreshed. That was a blessing to them, even if the Sheans saw them as a threat.

They would need someone to get them to Trost. From David's understanding, the reason that he could not hear his brother's thoughts were not because his brother was too far gone to save (that had yet to be seen), but rather, because the land of Shea existed on a plane outside of the time or reality of any other world. Only certain creatures could open the doorways between the dimensions. In this case, it was the elves. They had two choices before them. They could either enter the land and close the portal: that would mean that the gods and citizens of Shea would have to take their word for what they saw (unlikely), or they would have to leave a portal open so that Shiana could communicate what they saw back to David so that he could broadcast it to the gods. This was the one that he knew would be the only choice for the gods. Aqualon was the only one that would be able to open the portal. He had already expressed his concern at leaving the portal open. No creature in the history of Shea had ever even attempted to leave a portal open for an unknown amount of time. If it could even be done, it would be taxing on him, but he had agreed upon hearing the rest of their plan. David was thankful for this. It was a good plan, but there were many things that could go wrong. Almost too many things to chance it.

"But if we don't chance it, then what chance do we even have?" Shiana asked him.

"None," he said. "The Shadow has become too strong. It's devouring everything."

"Not if we can stop it, and even if we can't stop it, there has to be a way to save your brother."

David frowned and nodded. He remembered previous missions with that same goal, but none of them had ended well. He would have to somehow reach his brother through the Shadow. It was something he could not do. He had tried, but he could not get past the darkness, the sick and twisted horrors that he felt when he had tried to do that. It was overwhelming. Hopeless, and yet he had to keep trying.

"Even if you don't save him this time," said Shiana, "at least we have help. There must always be hope."

David reached out to pull her closer to him. "And this is why I love you." She smiled at him then, beaming, beautiful and brilliant, he thought.

When the time came for them to leave, they stood in the courtyard of Kialo's castle. Great, spiraling columns covered in vines rose above them. The gods stood close by, except Kristiniva, who was still uninterested in meetings of war. Aqualon asked them all to stand in a circle and hold hands. They did so, and then they watched in wonder as he wove the spell that opened the portal that transported them to Sark.

II. Xandra

Xandra was a mahldrusec, a creation of darkness and metal, killed by the Shadow and re-made by Shekley. He had been her boyfriend at the time, and she had volunteered to be the subject of his experiment. She had recently been sent on a mission to recover the lost parts of newly-made mahldrusecs and former hunters, Volkhan and Haz, who had been slain by a beast in the wilderness of Sark. She had hurried through the strange landscape, over black sand, up the rocky cliffs and through the trees and snows of the mountains to their location. Once there, she had been instructed to dig their bodies up from the ground, but there were no bodies, just parts in various states of frozen decay. She had hastily tied them together atop the body of Volkhan, who was the most well-preserved, and at least the most whole. She pulled the remains of the destroyed Mahldrusecs behind her, using rope that she had pulled from the corpse of the dead hunter Volkhan. She dragged them back to the citadel after retrieving them from the wilderness. It had taken her more time than she would have liked. She was quick and strong, but the island of Sark was vast. This mission had taken her hours. Hours that she should have been at the citadel protecting Shekley.

Finally, she had made it back. The massive doors of the main gate were open. She pulled the creatures behind her as she walked forward on the main roadway leading to the citadel.

She was greeted at the door by two of the animalistic creatures. They pulled the door open for her. She walked through the halls and took the stairs up to where she thought that she would find Shekley. She searched for him, but did not find him immediately. Instead, she came upon Darkhan, the foul man that claimed allegiance to the darkness. He had been the one that had helped them arrive, though they did not know it at the time. Xandra had seen how he animated the dead, and the disgusting way that he smiled as Shekley cut into them when the Shadow was hungry. Shekley was still the creator as far as the parts, but Darkhan could hold their souls in the void, and bring them back to the bodies, or hold them and still animate the bodies to do what he wanted. She wondered if things would have been different for her all those years ago if he would have been there to bring her back. But at that time there had only been Shekley, controlled by the Shadow, and her own desire to awaken. Thankfully, she still had her own soul. There was no one holding it hostage. Sometimes the Shadow would will her to do things, but only if done through Shekley. It was a programming feature that Shekley designed for her. She would only do what he told her to. She could not take orders from anyone else's voice.

So, unlike these new creatures, she could still feel. She held on to parts of her soul that Darkhan would otherwise control. She understood her actions enough to feel the guilt that came with them. The new creatures were more Shadow than beast now, and Darkhan held their souls even when they wanted to die. It was another way for the Shadow to grow in power.

Darkhan walked up to her now, his face hidden under a black hood, but his voice was deep and crisp, demanding attention when he spoke. "You brought them back...what's left of them," he observed, with a twisted laugh.

Xandra nodded. "They had already been buried and there was no sign of the beast."

He laughed deeper, amused at something that she could not understand. "Well, the god of life would have already hidden the beast, wouldn't he?" he asked.

Xandra just looked at him.

"Well, let me at them," he said, pushing her aside. He walked around her and stared down at the frozen carcasses of the dead hunters, and knelt down to them. He waived his hand and the fragments of Haz lifted into the air. With another wave, they flew through the nearby doorway and fell onto a table. Xandra noticed that the metal pieces didn't move. He brushed them aside and then reached out to Volkhan's blackened neck, where Galan had stabbed him with the holy kial flames. His fingers turned red when his skin made contact. He jerked his hands away quickly as smoke slowly lifted into the air from the wound. He laughed a deep chuckle.

"He did you in good, didn't he?" He laughed at the corpse. "I never saw it. You warned me, though." He laughed again, from deep within his chest. "I'll see to you," he said to the corpse, and with a wave of his hand, Volkhan's dead body rose into the air and floated behind Darkhan as the necromancer left Xandra standing alone in the hall. Xandra watched them go into the dimly lit room and then she left to find Shekley.

Xandra stared down at Shekley lying on the floor. He was weak and unconscious, thin and gaunt without his armor. His skin was a gray, pale color. His hair had grown out a little recently, but it was still short, and from the looks of it, wet with a cold sweat, a common thing when the Shadow left him. Clearly the Shadow had abandoned him for now. It scared her that she had been away, but she was glad that the Shadow was gone. She was not sure how long he had been lying here, needing her. She could sense that he was alive, but just barely, which was not unusual for him. The Shadow made sure of that. She reached out to him. She couldn't tell if he was sleeping or passed out. He seemed old and fragile. She lifted him up and carried him down the hall, to his bedroom, a place that the Shadow often didn't allow him to go. It was a place of peace and comfort for him, which she was sure that the Shadow despised. She tended to his wounds and hooked him to an IV. He would need the nourishment, she knew, because she had seen him like this before. In order to return him to full life, she would need to run fluids through him. Just when she thought she would have a moment of some peace, there was a knock at the door.

Xandra hesitated then walked to the door, jerking it open as one of the new creatures stared down at her. He was as strange-looking as the others. Part man, machine, and creature. She couldn't place what creature he was, because the animals from her own land had been extinct for some years now. She remembered having pets when she was a child, but nothing that looked like this. Huge, metal antlers protruded from his skull, which was misshapen...not exactly human, but not exactly animal either.

"Orders!" it demanded of her.

The Shadow must be coming back. It would delight in taking her away from Shekley right now.

"What orders?" she asked.

"From Nometheog, of course."

She stared at him.

"We are ready for your orders, commander. We have assembled as Darkhan commanded and we await your orders."

Xandra nodded. "I'm consulting with Shekley. Go back and wait with the others. I will be there when I'm told to be there." He saluted her and then turned to leave.

In truth, she had no idea what he was talking about, but something inside urged her to go with him. When the IV was running smoothly, she glanced down, grimacing at Shekley's pitiful state. When she was satisfied that there was nothing more that she could do, she left to command the new soldiers.

The gathering was full of the willing servants the Shadow had told Shekley about. They were the hunters of Sark, now twisted into the mechanical demons that resembled animals. Xandra realized that it was a fun but cruel trick to the god of darkness, who had turned them into the things that they had hated the most. They were either too naïve or dumb to see it, though.

Darkhan walked up behind Xandra, and placed a hand on her shoulder. She slapped it away.

"Commander," he greeted her, chuckling at her temper, "they await your orders and training." She could feel the twisted smile in his words, though his face was shielded by his black hood.

"I will teach them," she said.

He nodded in reply. "Nometheog has asked that I resurrect the rest of the bodies, but it will take some time. They are in pieces, and therefore, full animation will be difficult without Shekley's help.

"He is resting," she said, her gaze set straight ahead and her face set in defiance.

He nodded. "Of course," came his oily reply, "Still, I must be preparing. It will take a while to summon the power to animate them."

She waved a hand to dismiss him, concentrating on the creatures now lined up before her. She had trained before, but never creatures like this.

They waited for her, lined up as if for battle. She walked among them, taking in what they had become. Sloppy, she thought. Too organic, too close to something that thinks on its own. She felt a vanity in herself. Her ethereal sleekness outshined them all. Still, she had to see what they could do. She then set them into smaller groups and set rules for their fighting, then let them brawl, secretly hoping that some of them would be hurt beyond repair. She did not like Darkhan and something about giving him more work seemed satisfying in the pit of her gut. She wasn't sure if that was a feeling that came from her or from the Shadow. She stood back, watching them.

It was funny to her to watch them discover the things that were new to them. Most of them had never even tried

29

to use their new weapons, but she could tell that they had been good fighters before, and they enjoyed the destruction as much as her. They knew exactly how to aim to do the most damage. She pushed them to fight harder, and delighted in seeing their eyes wide with surprise as new weapons emerged. She let them fight until there was a clear winner in each group. She named them Seargents, tasked to command the smaller ranks. Then she ordered them to seek help for their wounds with Darkhan and be back whenever she summoned them. As soon as she finished the exercise and dismissed them, she left to care for Shekley, making sure to avoid Darkhan on her way up the stairs.

III. Through the Portal

Aqualon was able to bring the volunteers to Sark, close to the Eastern shore. Night had already settled, and a deep cold washed over the isle as stars swept the sky in a beautiful palette of distant light and the ocean roared to the east behind them. The selbdes shook in the cold, even though they wore clothes especially made for them by the finest elven tailors, and the gods had seen that they were completely equipped with what they thought they would need for Sark. The barren lands were especially brutal in the winter. No kial thieren trees grew there, it was miles of black sand beneath barren cliffs.

Aqualon stared out over the vast expanse of blackness; his face mirrored some distant memory. "It's a shame, what the gods did to Thiera. Sark was never the same after she fell." If there was a memory for them to see, the elf had blocked it from them with his own telepathy.

There was an awkward pause as he closed the portal. It had been agreed upon that the selbdes would telepathically contact him when they reached Trost or if there was any dire reason to while on their way to the city.

"I have to stay here and guard the portal," said Aqualon. "I need someone to stay here with me," he said

Shiana looked at her group, thinking on their abilities and how they might be useful. "Sassy, will you stay?" she asked.

"What? Why? I volunteered to go into the city, not stand around in a desert while the rest of you risk your lives"

"This is a risk, and I need the help," said Aqualon. "Nothing can cross into Shea without my knowledge. No elf has ever been asked to keep a portal open for more than the time admitted for travel between worlds. I will get exhausted. I will need someone to be vigilant, and to keep me from sleeping. It may not look like a lot, but it takes a lot of energy to keep this open."

Traegar nodded and placed a fist over her heart and bowed. "Thank you," said Aqualon. "It is much appreciated."

Shiana shot Sassy a stern look. Sassy rolled her eyes. "Fine. I'll stay," she said as she reached out to her dearest friend for an embrace. "Please be careful!" she insisted.

Shiana nodded, "You know that I always am." Shiana broke from Sassy and then stared into the distance with the others. It was hard to see anything. Both the sky and the sands were black here. Kim was already looking through the night vision binoculars that had survived in her pack.

"I can see it. From my calculations, I think it will take us a while to get there. We can reach it tonight, it's maybe ten miles. Maybe longer. There's a lot of sand to cross," she said. "I hope you're all up for a long walk tonight."

"Here, let me look," said Shiana, reaching out for the binoculars. She stared ahead. There was no mistaking the outline of Trost, dark and intimidating on the horizon, but she was not expecting it to be as completely dark as it was. When the city had been in Tahln, there had been lights to illuminate it during the night. As dark as the city was, there was still electricity to give it some bit of light, but it was not that way in this new land. The only way that it could be seen was because it was so much darker than the night sky, and there were lights, just not as many. Only a few burned high up in the citadel.

Shiana passed the binoculars back to Kim. "Okay," she said, with a deep sigh of dread, "I guess we need to get started. She started forward and the others followed. Soon the roar of the ocean was stifled into the sound of unrelenting wind.

The black sand of the desert at first seemed to be regular sand, just dark. It was soft and somewhat difficult to tread on, but as they walked, they saw that beneath the soft layer, there was a hard, smooth layer. The wind would blow the softer sand into hills and dunes, but then there would be the flat layer beneath. It seemed to be like rock, but there were jagged, red cracks, glowing throughout it, some deep, some shallow. As often as they could, they walked along the harder earth. It made for quicker travel. They moved forward without incident until they reached the gates of Trost.

Sassy watched her friends walk away until they were too far away for her to see, and then she pulled out her binoculars. When the figures got too far away to see clearly, she put the binoculars back and she looked at the elf. The portal was closed until they reached the city.

Aqualon sat silent, with a shell clutched to his ear, as if he were listening to something. It was a small whelk shell that he wore tied to his neck with a leather strap. Traegar was standing as still as a stone and the other two were not quite sure if she was in fact turning to stone. Sassy could not be as still, or as patient as the other two. She paced around in the frigid darkness. The wind whistled, lonely and howling, through the mountain passes and whipped the black sands into a frenzy around them.

Sassy's hands shook as she shivered and replaced the binoculars with night vision goggles from her pack. Her jacket was meant for cold desert nights, but it was colder here than she ever remembered it being in Tahln. When she got tired of pacing, she sat down again, huffing an impatient sigh.

Suddenly, a low, bass sound rumbled around them. She stopped and looked around, startled. She didn't think it was the wind. She stood and walked back to Aqualon. "Do you know what that was?"

He smiled. "Aye," he responded. She couldn't see his eyes. They were hidden under his hat.

"Well?" she asked impatiently.

"It was the call of a male valka beast," he responded calmly.

"What's a valka beast?"

He breathed in, thinking for a moment, "They're very large, four-legged beasts that roam the Sarkian wilderness.

They have large trunks, massive antlers, great white tusks, and black, shaggy fur."

Sassy sat down closer to the others as the call sounded again. It was soon answered by another close by.

"We don't have beasts where I'm from," she said, her voice shaking with both uncertainty and cold. "Well, we used to, but I haven't ever seen any that I remember."

Aqualon tried to imagine a land without beasts. He shook his head, he decided he couldn't.

"How long do you think they will be?" asked Sassy.

"I'm not sure. I'll give them the night at least. We should know if they get into trouble, though. If they do, then you and Traegar will go into the city. I'll wait here and if you're not back with them by nightfall tomorrow, then I will follow you. But if that is the case, then I will have to close the portal. I cannot leave it open while unattended.

Sassy nodded as the low rumble of the Valka's calls echoed around them. "That seems like a long time for me."

"It's not as long as it seems. Rest now, while you can," he said. "I'll know when they reach the city. That's when I'll need you the most. I'm not even sure that I can hold the portal open. I don't think that anyone has attempted a feat like this before." He placed the shell back to his ear and there was silence for a while. Sassy tried to lay down and sleep but the low, lonely sound of the Valka beasts awoke her every time that she dozed off. She took a deep breath and exhaled slowly. To pass time she paced and counted her steps all while imagining what she would do if she was in the city. She imagined the layout in her mind over and over and tried to imagine what she would do at each obstacle. She glanced at Traegar, convinced that she was completely turned to black stone, which matched the sand floor of the desert; complete with red, searing cracks running throughout her skin. Aqualon stayed seated, with the small

shell next to his ear.

IV. In the Darkness

The elf waited in the silence and the darkness. He did not know how long he had been here chained at his feet, on his knees, with his arms stretched out and chained at his sides. At first, he had been full of a rage and hatred, but that had turned to despair. He began to feel hunger and thirst that gnawed and twisted inside of him, knowing that the power of the goddess' spell had sealed his mouth shut so that even if he could get to food, there was no way to eat it. Hunger pangs gnawed at him constantly until the pain dissolved into sickness, then weakness. Now it was just numbness. The hunger didn't bother him, nor did any other physical pain, but the despair filled him.

He had fought with himself at first. The anger inside of him felt like a fountain welling up in his chest. After a while, though, it was stilled with his pains. What could he do? The reality was that the sky goddess had won her battle against him, but she had lost the war. His only consolation was that Celeste had escaped. Love was free again. If he never moved again, it was worth it, at least that's what he thought at first. Now the angel seemed as far away as his own life, his own mind.

It took him a long time, but he finally accepted it. Truth. It hurt, but it released him. Eventually there was not even pain. There was only dreams or numbness, and the absolute blackness of the cave, wrapping him in silence and dark solitude. He no longer felt anything with his physical body, though he could hear his own breathing and his own heartbeat, which had both become shallow and quiet. He didn't feel anything unless he was dreaming. That's how he began to understand the difference in his sleeping and waking. Feelings were just dreaming and numbness was waking.

He thought at times that he imagined seeing things, but then again, he may have dreamed it. He could no longer tell if he was asleep or awake. Sometimes he thought that he heard water dripping, but then again, it was probably imagined. After a while, he began to think all things were imagined. Even his numbness and his dreams were starting to mold into the same thing. He began to forget things, important things, confusion was taking over whenever he did try to remember anything at all. After enough days in the silent darkness, he began to forget everything including his self. He began to forget why he was here and where he was.

Sometime, there was no way to tell time in this cursed cavern, he was startled when he heard a voice speaking to him. It was deep, and growling, but soft and whispering at the same time. A woman's voice. "Wouldn't you want to feel something right now? Anything?"

He pondered what he heard. Was it even real? He only nodded his head, or so he thought. He had forgotten what that felt like, and he was still unsure of whether he was asleep or awake. The voice must have perceived his intention.

"I can help you feel." The elf attempted to look, but he saw nothing. There was the same complete darkness, stillness, and loneliness as before.

"Do you know who I am? Everyone knows me, but they despise me. Everyone abuses me. They take my gift and twist it. I am present at birth and death. I follow each one of you through life. Nometheog chains me, so that his void can remain pure, but I find ways to escape. Khanhine could not kill without me. Saigolai has yet to create something that I don't purify in birth. Even his angel's gain their power through me. Sari would not exist without my gifts. Selfirin and Luna couldn't create without me. What is the light without the pain of a burning sun? What is creation without the pain of work, and thought? The other gods find ways to discredit me, but I am always here."

"Vishka, goddess of pain and suffering!" He realized it, but he could not say it.

"I think you will appreciate my gift. You haven't felt for so long. Wouldn't it be nice to feel?" the goddess asked. Her voice sounded excited, and somehow comforting.

The numbness left him then, and he felt something then. Pain. Excruciating, crippling, unbearable pain like he had not felt before as the bones in his hands were broken and he fell forward, his body slamming onto the cold, hard stone of the cave's floor. He felt tears in his eyes both from the pain and the thought that he was now free. There was a loud cracking of bones and breaking of silence as his feet were also pulled free. He couldn't yell, his voice had been stolen, and although he hurt beyond anything he had imagined

45

before, the pain was empowering. It was a purifying pain from the goddess herself. It made him know that he was not a dream, and he was remembering himself.

"I think that you will use my gift wisely. I, too, hate the sky goddess. Of course, if not for her, I would not be able to be here. She summoned Nometheog, and I escaped again." The elf felt a scratching sensation on his back where her claws tried to comfort him. "If you feel me, you are still alive! Though, whether you are dreaming or not, I do not know. I don't dream. I just watch and intercede. There is no sleep for me." She was silent for a moment and then her voice sounded farther away as she left him. "Remember me, Arik!" Her words were like a knife tearing away a veil of confusion. He had forgotten himself because his name was being forgotten... "Remember my gift to you. Nometheog will no doubt chain me again, and soon."

Arik's breathing was heavy and labored, and tears flowed freely from his eyes. His broken bones were all he could feel at the moment, but he tried to concentrate on what the goddess had said. As he lay there, he began to remember himself, his life. He remembered reality and his hatred for Kristiniva. He was remembering his name. Even it had escaped him while he was in the darkness. He was alive now, and free. Movement would be slow to come to him, but it would come. He lay, silently weeping for a very long time, or so it seemed. When he could bare the pain enough to move, he inhaled a deep breath and felt the stone of the cavern beneath him. He concentrated on the sound of the water drops he had been hearing. He realized they were not a dream. Maybe it was a way out. Using his knees and his arms, he felt his way through the pain, shaking weakly as he slowly scraped himself over the rocks and followed the sound.

V: The Feast

Celeste was the rightful queen of Sark, wronged by her own subjects and imprisoned by the sky goddess in a land far from her own for seven years. She had returned only to find that Sark had fallen and suffered in her absence, and her husband, Victor, had been left powerless without her. She had recently left with him on a mission to find any subjects that would declare loyalty to her. The war started here, and she would see it end here. Upon gaining her power back, her husband had received his as well. Now they would have to take Sark back from the evil that had run rampant while she was away.

Her first stop had been at a meeting with the tavern owner, Saltook, who had stayed loyal the many years that she was away. They had the werewolves and khanhine-lupa aiding them, which was a great relief. Now, she was meeting with the Scithronians, a band of thieves that were orphaned children of Sark before Celeste was kidnapped. She had seen that they were fed, housed, and educated. It was a top priority as queen. But when she had been enslaved, and the palace was attacked, the children were left to run and hide from the hunters that now controlled the land. They had banded together in resistance, forming their own tribe, led by a gifted seer named Klarissa.

Celeste was now in their den, looking at Arista, the princess of the moon elves, in disbelief. She trembled at the news that the elf princess had delivered to them, but the questions forming in her head left her feeling dizzy. Arik had saved her from Kristiniva, and reunited her with her husband. Now his sister was telling her that he had been stripped of his birthright and banished from Shea, name and all. The look on the princess' face left her heartbroken. She had immediately reached out to her and asked for privacy to speak to the elf princess alone. Klarissa had been quick to show them to a quiet room away from the others. They sat in the simple room, carved into the rocks and roots underneath the forest of Sark. Despite the cold outside, and the emotional turmoil filling the gaps in air, the rooms felt warm and inviting.

The angel looked at Arista, her lips quivering as she spoke. "Tell me everything. I have to know. I am the cause of this and I must make it right."

Arista nodded, with tears filling her eyes. She told Celeste everything. "I knew what we risked when we started," she said. "I knew that banishment or death could happen, but what she has done to him is far worse than either. She has erased his name, and she has stolen the moon from him...that is a horror that I cannot imagine. She has taken the one thing that isn't hers to take."

"Help me understand, Arista, how can she take the moon from him?" Arista shook her head.

"I'm not sure. I wish it was as simple as death, not that I wish death on my brother, but the gods are known for handing out punishments that make death seem kind. I have spoken to the quirials and they tell me that she sealed his mouth so that he could not speak, and she took his telepathy so that he could not communicate with us. But the one thing that gives me hope is that I know for a fact that he was brought here. I..." tears streamed down her face at the guilt-driven memory. "I was commanded to bring him here." She was so overcome with emotion that it took her several more minutes to collect herself. Celeste reached out and drew the princess to her in a comforting and quick embrace.

"We're going to make it right," Celeste reassured.

"I knew that if I didn't do as she said, then the same thing would happen to me, and I knew that if it did, that I would never see him again. I did it, knowing instantly that I would banish myself and find him."

Celeste had shed her own tears as she heard the story. "I know her ways and how hard it is to escape her wrath." Celeste fought back memories of her own imprisonment. "I never thought I would think it, but Victor is right. He should have killed her."

Arista shook her head. "No, never say that," she said. "There are binding laws for a reason. Victor did what he was sent to do. He got back what she stole from you, and he got you back home.

"But he couldn't have done it without your brother."

"I will find him," she said.

"I know you will, because we will help you." Celeste embraced the elf again, feeling her desperation, and the tears falling on her shoulder. "We must!" she whispered.

Arista only nodded, then pulled away as she wiped away her tears. "Shall we get back to your subjects?" she asked the angel. "They are overjoyed at your return," she said as she handed Celeste a white cloth. "I don't mean to take that from them or from you."

Celeste looked at the cloth. She had seen a similar one in Shea. Arik had given it to her to wipe away her tears of sorrow. Arista now gave it to her for the same reason. Dark angels often wept blood when their sorrows were overwhelming. The cloth made the blood vanish. She wondered if it had other uses as well. After she wiped her tears, the two women collected themselves and joined the Scithronians for the feast.

The Scithronians honored them and there was enough food brought by the elves to feed all of them for several days. Celeste made a toast to the endurance of the Scithronians. She spent as much time speaking to each of them individually as she could. They were each special to her. Before the kingdom fell, she often spent time seeing to their needs herself. They were her children before she had birthed her own. Now, they were what was left of the old kingdom. They had prepared music, stories, and tricks of entertainment, so the feast had several courses and lasted for many hours.

Angelik grew tired and was soon sleeping on her mother's lap. Alexandria was trading tips and tricks with the young thieves and swapping stories of valor. Celeste, Victor, Carmina, Klarissa, and Arista had pulled out the maps and were discussing strategy when Victor was summoned outside. One of the thieves who had been on guard duty bowed to his king and asked him to come see what he had found. Victor shrugged away Celeste's worried look as he followed the boy and climbed the ladder out into the bitter cold of a Sarkian night.

VI. The Dark City of Trost

When Shiana looked up at the city, she got a feeling of complete despair. She always did, but this time it was different. Even for Trost, there seemed to be some new feeling of foreboding doom coming from within the city of black metal.

Normally, there were sentries posted at the gates, but not only was there no one there, the doors to the massive gates stood ajar. Some part of her was glad, but another part of her was wary. Maybe because it seemed too easy. She led the group inside. After telepathically communicating to Aqualon to open the portal, she began sending David her thoughts and visions of what was happening, so that he could show it to the gods.

When they were through the gates, Kim halted them for a moment. "Shiana, I think we should take the access ladders. I think there are sentries at the citadel entrance."

"Good idea," Shiana responded. "It will be easier to sneak in that way."

Trost was a city built on levels that descended into the ground. It reached to about four-thousand feet below. There were mines near the bottom, but the selbdes had never been there themselves. Upon entering the city, one could stand at the gates, and straight ahead was a road leading to the citadel, which towered another two-thousand feet to the sky, with buildings for agriculture and education spanning the distance around it. Behind the citadel were the farms that fed the city. The main road was connected by two others which intersected the main road and paralleled the front of the citadel. On either side of the main road one could look out and see the tops of buildings, some more than four-thousand feet tall. There were various platforms, roads, and transit systems that were built between the buildings, but there were only two ways to reach the lower levels. The first way was through the citadel, which had elevators and platforms that could access any level. The other way was the emergency access ladders, which were usually only used by maintenance workers, but they also allowed escape in the instance of emergencies and mass evacuation. There were access platforms every two-hundred feet that led to the roads, stairs, and other pathways through the city. Shiana was hoping to reach the first one.

"I hope you're ready for this," she said as they neared the ladder. She hated ladders even more than elevators. She prepared herself, then edged her way down.

Shiana stared below her, though she knew that she should not have looked down. With the electricity out, she stared down into a black abyss. Her hands were sweating, and she felt dizzy and nauseous.

"*Don't fall*!" she thought over and over.

"*You've got this*!" she heard encouragement from David and it made her feel better. After hesitating for longer than she knew she should, she looked above her. Michael was looking down at her from the top of the ladder.

"We can find another way," he said. Shiana shook her head.

"No," she insisted. "I've got this!" She shakily began to slowly lower herself down the ladder, one rung at a time, the cold metal feeling like slippery ice in her hand. She was determined, though. There were too many lives at risk to fail now. Michael and Teri followed her down with James and Kim next. Iluma floated down beside them, casting a pale light for them to see by.

When she finally set her foot on the stable platform at the bottom of the ladder, she breathed a sigh of relief then sat down. Both exhaustion and the cold that wrapped around the city made her shiver uncontrollably. She looked out at the city, or what she could see of it, stretching out before her. Normally, it was lit up with lights and there was the noise of the workers moving about and the citizens going about their day, but there were only a few lights shining from the citadel. Everything else was cold and eerily quiet, which was something that was terrifying, even for Trost.

She pulled water from her pack and took a large gulp, then wiped her mouth on her sleeve. She waited for the others to descend. Michael came down next and sat beside her.

"I've never seen it this dark," he said.

"Or felt this cold," Teri finished his thought.

James and Kim were quiet. They sat down to rest. After a while, Shiana spoke, "I'm glad we didn't try to go through the citadel. It would have been too risky. If there's no power, then there's a good chance that the elevators are not working."

"It also means that the ventilation system is probably shut off," said Kim.

"And that explains the silence," said James. "They're probably all dead by now...suffocation..." he crawled to the edge of the platform and gazed into the darkness. He wasn't sure what he was searching for. Perhaps it was some sign of life, a sound, a light, anything that showed hope. But if there was anything there, he could not sense it with his mind.

"Even if everyone from the top layers made it out, there's was no hope for those on the lower levels," he reasoned.

The fairy landed on Teri's shoulder and spoke her native language to the selbdes. When she finished, Teri interpreted.

"She says that if we tell her where we need to go, then she will scout ahead."

Shiana nodded. "First road, two blocks ahead, make a right. There's a building at the end of that road. That's the one my office was in. That's where we are going." Teri told the fairy what Shiana had said, then the fairy dimmed her light and flitted away.

Kim looked at Shiana, "So when are you going to speak to David?" she asked.

Shiana smiled. "I'm already speaking to him. The gate is open. The gods can see what I see."

"Have they said anything?"

Shiana shrugged. "I'm not sure. David has not told me if they have."

They waited for Iluma to come back. The fairy brightened herself so that they could see her better. She spoke, and Teri once again interpreted. "She says everything is dark. It appears to be locked, so she doesn't know how we can get in."

Kim was the first to stand. "Since there's no power, there will be no alarm. We can just break a window."

The others stood and followed her. Iluma led the way, shining light where Kim stepped. The others followed. Their steps echoed loudly, bouncing off the hollowness of the dark city around them. They followed the second walkway to the building that Shiana had worked in. When they got to the building, Kim wrapped her fist in her sleeve and punched out the window beside the door. The sound of shattering glass echoed through the city.

"This is the only good thing about losing power," Kim said. The window was as tall as the door, so it was easy for them to walk through the opening into the building.

"Follow me," Shiana said. They walked forward. The main entrance was a large, open space designed with a high roof made of glass to filter sunlight through, but now it was just black mirrors. On three sides there were offices with glass panels and glass doors.

"We have to take some stairs," said Shiana.

"Lead the way," said Michael.

"My office can be a safe space while we're here," Shiana said, as she led them further down.

When they reached the room, they rested again. The air had become thick and sleepy feeling.

"Shiana, we can't stay here for long, the ventilation isn't working," said Kim. "I vote that we chance the citadel. The few lights that we saw were coming from there, which means that they probably have power, working vents, and that's where we will end up anyway."

Shiana nodded. "Yes, we will go there next. I had to bring you all here, though. You can't see it now in the darkness, but the machine he built that did this is in the square. I could see it outside the window." She peered out of the window now, but it was useless. There was only darkness.

"We need to go now," she said, "but if anything happens to any of us, and for some reason we can't make it out of the city, then this is a safe place to lay low until you can escape."

They decided not to linger for too long. Kim and Iluma would be leading them, since Iluma seemed to be the only source of light, and Kim could see what was going to happen before it happened. Shiana and Michael would follow, and Teri and James would close the back of the group. Together, they walked carefully out of the building and back to the access route that would take them to the citadel.

"When we get inside, someone will need to get the vents working," said Shiana. "We're going to need my office if something goes wrong."

"I'll go," Kim volunteered. She looked at the fairy, "will you assist me?"

Iluma emitted a musical tone and flew over to land on Kim's shoulder.

"No," Shiana said as she shook her head. "Teri should go. She can understand the language of the machines, and if Iluma goes with her, then they can communicate more clearly."

Teri nodded with the agreement. "I can do it," she said.

"Meet us back here." Shiana said. "Unless we tell you different."

"Let's go," said Shiana. The other selbdes and the fairy then made their way out of the building and towards the citadel.

VII. The Tree

Arik did not know how far he had pulled himself, or even which direction he was headed in. He went towards what he thought was the dripping water, but now he wasn't so sure. It seemed like the sound was getting more faint. Maybe he was dreaming again, but no, he couldn't be. He couldn't go forward any more. There was something in front of him. He reached his arm up to feel. It felt like more stone on the wall of the cavern. He shook with pain and he felt he could go no further. He decided that he would sleep now, but sleep did not come. The wall was moving, it seemed. He smelled the air, trying to gather reasoning. It was the smell of a kial tree. If there was a tree here, then he couldn't be far from the outside. The idea was overwhelming to him. He reached out trying to feel the tree roots with the inside of his arm. His hands were too broken to be of any help. He missed his telepathy. The trees had a lovely language, and if he could speak to it, he was sure that it could help him.

He didn't know if maybe the tree had telepathy. Perhaps it could understand him, though he couldn't speak to it. After a few moments of no response, he began to get discouraged. No matter, if the tree didn't care to help him, then he would find another way. He took a while to listen, and then he made a right turn against the stones and roots and crawled along beside of them. Using his elbows and knees, he scraped himself forward again, only somewhat aware that his clothes had become baggy and thread bare as he moved forward. Then he heard it again. The sound of the dripping water was close by. He moved towards the sound with new hope. There was then another sound and for a moment he thought of Vishka, but he realized that the tree had heard him. There was a loud rumbling that shook the stones beneath him as the roots of the tree twisted and shifted the rocks around him. Rocks began to fall from above him, he stopped, hoping that one did not crush him. When the rumbling and the noise stopped, dust started to settle, and then there was light and deep, cold air sweeping into the open space of the cave. The light was almost blinding at first. Thankfully, it was the light from the stars. The moon did not shine, but the sky was bright. The smell of roots, and trees, and even animals wafted in on the breeze. If he could have laughed, he would have. The space was small, but he could fit through it. He moved forward slowly, and scraped over more rock, which soon turned to snow and soft, black dirt under an open sky. He rolled onto his back to gaze up at the bright lights. He never remembered the stars looking so bright and lovely before. It was such a welcome sight after being in the darkness for so long. He smiled silently as he gazed up at the heavens, thankful to the goddess Vishka, who had done him such a grand favor. Then he missed Luna. Where was the moon? Where was Luna? He needed her light now more than ever. The stars were lovely, but Luna gave him life, and light, and healing. Perhaps it was a new moon. He had lost track of time. No matter. Any light was better than the darkness of the cavern. He chanced the last of his energy to find a warm, soft place to lay under a kial tree, perhaps the same one that had saved him. He let the warmness fill him with comfort and then he really did sleep and dream, and it was the first time in a while that he was sure it was a dream.

He awoke to a blinding, painful light of day. The sun burned his skin and he hid beneath the roots of the tree, which opened up for him. It took a while for his eyes to adjust and his headache to go away. When he could open his eyes without unbearable pain, he saw the tracks where he had dragged himself away from the cave, lined with his blood.

He looked down at his body, unrecognizable to him. His skin was dark gray, and he saw that his bones jutted out at odd angles, his hands and feet were black, purple, and swollen. He had lost some of his clothes in the cave and what he now wore was ragged and hanging off of him. Scrapes and scratches bled from various points all over his body, and he could still feel the burning from Vishka's claws on his back. His long, black hair was no more. Instead, dry, brittle, white hair hung down his back. if he could have seen his own eyes, then he would have seen yellow where there had been purple before. He sighed as he came to the realization that he needed help. There was no way that he could make it back to Shea. He would need healing first. Healing was possible, he thought, but only with endless dust. He had given all of his dust to Celeste. He had to figure out where he was. He had to get to the king's castle and find the dust that he had given to the angel. He said a prayer now, to Saigolai. Usually, he saved such things for Luna, but she was no help to him right now. But life, Saigolai, he would

answer. He had to.

VIII: Fletcher

Victor looked down at the hunter before him, bound on his knees by two of the Scithronians: Morten, a small-framed blonde boy, and Vaska, a broad-shouldered brunette girl. The dark angel peered at the hunter and perceived his soul was a darkened, muddy brown. The boy looked up to him, a scowl on his face.

"He said he was looking for you," said Morten.

"We figured it would be best to bring him directly to you, though we found those on him," Vaska said, motioning with her head towards a pile of weapons that lay on the ground.

"You missed one," said Victor. As he knelt on one knee before the hunter, Morten tugged harder on the rope as the hunter struggled and gave an involuntary grunt. Victor unsheathed a hunting knife from the man's belt and threw it into the pile with the others.

"Fletcher," he said, still kneeling, level with the hunter's face. "You were looking for me, but you didn't really want to see me."

Fletcher shook his head. "I thought we got rid of you."

Victor let out a quick agitated sigh, part amusement and part bitterness. "Almost," he said. "You hurt me. You hurt me in ways that you can never imagine, but I'm not as easy to kill as the people of Saletu." His voice was smooth and unnervingly calm.

Fletcher turned pale at his words.

Victor nodded, knowingly. "I know what you did, Fletcher, but it's always good to hear a confession and clear any misunderstanding."

"I just did what I was told. I was following orders."

"Excuses!" Victor exclaimed, his voice giving away his anger. "I'm already tired of them."

He paused for a moment, shaking his head, his eyes closed as he searched for what he needed. There was an abundance of power for him throughout Sark. He did not have to travel to grasp it. There were so many wailing spirits that had gone without justice for too long.

"Can you imagine it?" he said, opening his eyes.

Fletcher stared at him, blankly.

"Can you?" he asked.

The hunter shrugged.

Victor reached out to the hunter's arm and pulled up his sleeve, revealing the brand of the hunters on his forearm.

"Did it hurt?" he asked.

"Not too bad," he said.

"Imagine it, not just there, but all over, inside of you, and there's nowhere to go." He placed a hand on the hunter's forehead. "Just imagine it," he said.

Fletcher's heart suddenly raced in fear and panic. Then where Victor's hand touched him, he felt it, heat from the flames. Smoke smoldered beneath the angel's hand and Fletcher let out an involuntary scream. Victor pulled his hand away. Fletcher's forehead bled with the imprint from the burn.

"I only locked the doors. I was told to lock them. I… if I didn't, I would have been in there with them. Do you think I could really go against Darkhan's will?" Fletcher was shouting. "He would have done worse than kill me."

Victor hit him then in the jaw with the back of his fist. Fletcher winced in pain as blood poured from within his mouth and the side of his face momentarily sizzled with fire. "Out with it," he demanded, his voice an angry growl, "you did more than lock the doors!" Victor stood, staring down at what he thought was a pitiful sight, as the man sought for some escape, some excuse, but found none.

Fletcher felt himself as one of the people dying in Saletu, locked inside the buildings with no escape as the fires burned hotter around him, clinging to loved ones with no consolation for their safety and every hope of escape was answered with more fire and more smoke.

Tears ran from his eyes as he screamed and coughed with the memory of the smoke, as if he were there inhaling it.

Fletcher only nodded at first, as the vision passed, still reeling from his pain. "I did it," he coughed, gasping for air. "I gathered the people up. I helped the others force them inside the buildings, and I threw in a torch."

Victor nodded. "Better," he said, gazing down at the hunter. His eyes made the hunter shudder.

"You have caused a lot of people a lot of pain, some of it unforgivable. But I am a merciful king, and I will allow you to right some of the wrong that you have done to my kingdom. Those people, the ones that died in the fire, they cannot get back their lives, but you have a chance to build a new life. A prosperous life for yourself and others. You will help rebuild Saletu. You sought me out because of the kial brew at The Howling Wolf. It drew you to me, so that I could give you a chance to right your wrongs, but to do so, you must swear loyalty to me. In doing so, you will betray the hunters, but also be under my protection. The fact that you were at the Howling Wolf, instead of the fortress in the barren lands, shows that there is something within you worth saving. If you swear loyalty and then break your word, or if you refuse your just punishment of rebuilding Saletu, then I will know. If I sense a hint of disloyalty, then you will die in the same way that the people of Saletu died. Can you swear your allegiance to me here, now?"

Fletcher nodded his head.

"Then say it," said the angel.

"I...am loyal to you. I will do as you wish and rebuild Saletu." The hunter spoke the words, though it seemed to cause him physical discomfort to do so.

"You will refer to me as your king from henceforth."

"Yes, my king," said Fletcher as he stared the angel in the eyes, unable to pull his gaze away.

Victor nodded, then turned to the scithronians grasping the restraints. "Let him go," he said.

When the ropes loosened, Fletcher fell to the ground, recovering his strength. When he had collected himself, he bowed properly before his king.

Victor stared down at him for a moment and then spoke, "Your first duty to me is to go to the fallen castle. I will meet you there," he said.

Fletcher nodded.

"If you go anywhere else first, then I will know it. Do not stray from your path."

Fletcher nodded again.

"Go now, and do not stop until you've reached the fallen castle."

"Yes, my king," Fletcher said. Then he got to his feet and headed towards the castle at a full run.

Victor turned to the scithronians. "Thank you," he said to them. They each bowed to him and then they gathered the weapons left by the hunter.

"What should we do with these?" Morten asked.

"Do as you wish with them," he said. "He will not need them any longer. Not for now, anyway," he said. Then he turned and walked back towards the feast.

Chapter IX: The Citadel

The group walked on in silence with only the sounds of the wind racing through the streets and alleys. The wind was stronger here than it had been in Tahln, and the direction changed often. Every now and then, trash would rustle around and blow near them, startling them with the sound. They would be relieved at the sight of just a newspaper rustling by a window or an abandoned cup rolling along the ground. Finally, they reached the outer edges of the citadel. The dark, black building towered above them, dwarfing anything else around them, and making the chasm that the rest of the city was built in look deeper and darker. They said their goodbyes to Teri and Iluma, who needed to go in a different entrance, and then they continued forward through a loading dock. There were trucks parked in rows and crates of various sizes stacked around. Some of the trucks had been turned on their sides. There were scorch marks, signs of a fire around some of the trucks.

"What happened here?" asked Shiana.

"I did," said Michael with a wry chuckle. "This is where I got David out the last time, and you know," he said, "sometimes I get carried away."

Shiana nodded. "I guess traveling through the portal made Shekley forget about the cleanup."

"Well, it's not like there's many people left to do the cleaning," responded James.

There was silence then for a moment as they traveled towards the entrance. They were on alert, because if there were lights in the citadel, then that meant that there were creatures as well.

Shiana spoke to the others telepathically. *"We need to find Shekley,"* she said. *"That's our main task. We need to know what he's planning. Don't engage the creatures unless we have to."*

Now Kim spoke, *"Hide. I sense them already. There are two coming."*

The selbdes quickly found cover as they slid between small spaces in the crates and between the crates and the wall. A door on the wall to their left opened and between the cracks in the crates, they could see two extremely tall, large creatures that appeared to be made out of metal and something else. Were they animals? It had been many years since any of the selbdes had seen any animal that was alive in Tahln. Yet, here they were, well, something of the sort.

The first one spoke with a growling voice that echoed through the loading dock in a roar.

"Clean up!" he growled. "We have all this power and we're told to clean up like some ragged bar maid!"

Shiana wanted to punch herself for speaking too soon about Shekley forgetting the cleanup.

"Whatever it takes to prove ourselves," the other responded. He motioned for the other one to help him and together they pushed one of the wrecked freight trucks upright.

"Do you realize what we could be doing with these?" The hunter looked at the large, metal paws that had replaced his hands.

"What? You want to wrestle a bear with your bear hands?" the other asked.

A growl that shook the crates that the selbdes were hiding behind erupted from the bear.

"You're not as witty as you think, Fox!" He shouted at the other and landed a blow against another truck, which he then sat upright without the other's help. Thankfully, they were moving farther from the doorway that they had entered through.

"Let's go," said Kim, telepathically. *"We've only got a small opportunity here."*

"That's a warehouse inside. We should be able to hide, but I don't think we will be alone," she said, *"so, move fast!"*

One by one, they ran into the door, and quickly found hiding spots. There were none of the animalistic creatures, but the workers were definitely mahldrusecs. They were cleaning up crates and debris. The ceiling had apparently fallen in, probably a result of the travel through space and time. There were mahldrusecs, some of them flying with wings, others used propulsion systems, hovering at the ceiling, working to repair it. The ones with wings gave off soft, electrical humming sounds. The selbdes made a plan as they tried to creep through the stacks of crates and machinery, edging closer to the doors that led inside the citadel. When they were all close enough to chance making it through the doors, Kim spoke in their minds.

"First door on the right," she said, as they crept forward slowly. They squeezed through the unlocked door and ran forward through a dark hall lit with battery operated lights. Michael ran first, followed by James, then Shiana, and Kim in the rear. Shiana could hear the creatures behind her, but did not think that they had been spotted.

She saw Michael and James run into a door on their right. She slipped in as quietly as she could behind them, immediately followed by Kim. It was the stairwell. It was darker than the hall, but there were emergency lights lighting each landing. They quietly began the ascent towards the top. "Do any of you sense Shekley yet?" Shiana asked.

"No, but I can still hear the thoughts of the creatures cleaning back there," said Michael.

The others heard the same. They began climbing the stairs then. It was a long climb. They stepped up endlessly it seemed, not sure of how long it was taking them. It was darkness, quiet, and the repeated rhythm of footsteps until Shiana suddenly stopped and crouched down on the stairs. "I can't go any more," she said. "It's taking all of my energy to speak to David through this far of a distance, while seeking out Shekley at the same time. I just can't go any more."

James helped her stand, "We'll find a place to rest on the next landing," he said. "It's not safe to stop here." Then the group moved forward, Kim in the front, James and Shiana in the middle with Michael watching their backs. When they got to the next landing, Kim peeked through the doorway into the hall, then closed the door back and looked to the others. "We're in the medical halls," she said. Shiana nodded, realizing that the number on the floor was twenty-six. They still had a long way to go. The top of the citadel was 170 stories above ground.

They followed Kim through the door, and then down a hall, past an elevator. At the moment, the hall seemed to be abandoned.

Kim looked into one of the rooms. "This one looks clean," she said.

"All the fate of the world is hinged on us surviving this and you're worried about a clean room," noted Michael.

Kim shrugged. "The little things matter too," she said. Shiana lay on the bed and then she slept for a while. The others kept watch.

"They sat mostly in silence while Shiana slept, but they were constantly reaching out for any sign of Shekley. Eventually, Michael slept in the chair next to the bed, and

Kim leaned against the door, barring it, just in case someone had the key to the lock.

James stared out of the window. There was still darkness, but then he heard a voice.

"James," it said his name. A deep, smooth, clear voice.

"Did you all hear that?" James asked.

Kim had been concentrating hard on trying to see what would be happening that it had drowned out all the other voices around her. Michael and Shiana were both sleeping.

"What is it?" Kim asked.

James shook his head. "It's not Shekley, but someone said my name." He shrugged. "I don't know, maybe someone else is named James here.

"Maybe you should rest, too," Kim said. "I don't even know if Shekley would know your name. He's too hellbent on capturing David and Shiana to really bother with the rest of us, unless he sees us coming.

James shrugged, "Like I said, maybe someone else is named James."

Kim nodded. "Maybe," she said, trying not to worry.

Shiana rested, and when she awoke, they continued up the stairs. As they got closer to the top, they could begin to hear more thoughts and more movement in the halls. They ascended the stairs as quietly as they could, but just before reaching the fifty-fifth floor, Kim cursed and drew her guns from her holsters, and the door on the landing directly below them opened.

"Run!" she ordered, speaking telepathically. Shiana and James ran forward to the next landing and stepped through the door, but then there was an explosion. They fell forward. Smoke slid out from the cracks around the door. Shiana ran back to aid the others but before she could touch the door, she heard a muffled cry from James, and felt a sudden severe pain on the back of her head before she blacked out.

X. The Power Station

Teri and Iluma had gone into a side door of the citadel. It led to the halls for maintenance and would lead to the core of the city's power, or at least a power station that could direct them to it. They traveled side-by-side, Iluma lighting the way. They found that talking to each other was easy, because of Teri's gift.

"I just need to get to the central power source," Teri said. "Once there, it shouldn't be too hard to restore the power. I know that the city is powered from a radioactive mineral found in the mines. In the other world, we had satellites and computers that helped maintain everything, but I don't think this place has any of that. So, the crystal has probably overpowered itself and possibly overloaded everything. The problem is that if the mineral is damaged, then I don't know if I can fix it. Probably, a lot of the city was actually damaged from the movement between space and time. Possibly even the mines and the power supply. Do you follow me?" she asked the fairy.

"I think so," said the fairy. "For what it matters, I do."

"Good," she said. There was silence for a while as they moved quietly down halls, closer to the center of the citadel. They moved down stairs and ladders, avoiding any creatures that they passed along the way, until they reached the room that she needed. The door was locked. A panel sat next to it. She assumed it was for a fingerprint.

"Damnit!" Teri exclaimed. "I can't open it. Not only would I need a fingerprint, but I would need the power to be working to get in. She gave the large, metal door a hard kick. "Who makes a door to the power room that only opens if you have power?" she thought out loud.

"There has to be another way," reasoned Iluma. "You are right. No one would do that."

Teri shook her head. "I don't know of another way in. This is the door that leads to everything important in this building."

The two sat thinking for a moment, not sure how to get out of the situation, but then Teri had an idea. "You're right, Iluma. There is another way. There has to be some tool that can open this door. I don't know what it is, but we are going to find it. I'm guessing that it would be with the maintenance workers, so any maintenance room should have one. There's one not far from here."

After back-tracking a couple of floors, they found a maintenance door. It was locked, but easily opened with the right amount of force. It was one of the only doors that was locked with an old-fashioned key. They rifled through various tools. Some of them were old fashioned and others were newer and seemed more complicated. Teri picked up a large gun-shaped instrument that glowed with a blue light.

"What is that?" asked Iluma.

"It's some sort of weapon. I think," responded Teri. "I'm going to hold on to it, just in case we need it. Though, it's not what I'm looking for. I'm assuming that for now, if I could find some way to back up the lock to a battery, then it should open."

"What's a battery?" the fairy asked.

"I'll know it when I see it." She rounded a corner and saw that the room opened up to a much larger area. Larger machinery lay around in various stages of repair. Iluma let out a horrified sigh, and Teri looked across the room to see the body of a man lying on the floor, a tool still gripped in his hand. There was no mistaking that he had been deceased for some time. Teri found a tarp and laid it over the man's body.

"He was an ordinary worker," she said. "There are a lot of those here, probably all like him, but it explains why no one else has gotten the door open." She walked over to examine some of the equipment.

"Here we go," she said, "I found a battery. I just hope we can make it work," she said. She found a bag of tools and rifled through it, pulling out screwdrivers. "All this high-tech stuff and they still haven't replaced a good 'ol flathead." She smiled. "Sometimes simplicity is best."

She emptied out the bag of the rest of its contents and filled it with only the things that she needed, and the gun.

"Let's go," she said. The fairy nodded back and led the way back to the fingerprint lock.

Teri examined it by Iluma's light and unscrewed a panel on the bottom of the device. Then, she popped the battery into place. Soon, there were beeping sounds and lights glowing on the screen.

"It wants a fingerprint," she said.

"How do we get one?" asked the fairy.

"Well, if I were a regular human, I would go chop the finger off of that dead maintenance man, but thankfully, I'm not human. This is a machine, and all machines talk. I just have to figure out its language."

She closed her eyes and placed her finger on the entry pad. At first, a computerized male voice told her "access denied," but after a few attempts, a different beeping sound was heard and the voice said, "welcome, administrator," and the door slowly slid open. Teri left one hand on the entry pad and pushed the bag of tools in-between the sliding doors just in case they decided to close.

She smiled as she looked at Iluma, "Let's go," she said. They stepped into the vast room. They couldn't see much. It seemed darker here than in the rest of the citadel. Teri went forward, feeling with her hands. Even Iluma's light was not quite enough to make out what was in front of her. She could feel the fairy shaking on her shoulder.

"Are you afraid?" she asked.

"More than ever," the fairy responded. Their speech echoed in the vast chamber. Finally, Teri felt something in front of her.

"This must be the place," she said.

"I think I can give us more light," the fairy said, "but it won't last long and if I do this, then I will be very weak afterwards."

"No," said Teri. "No, I think we've found the crystal, but it is as I feared. The crystal itself is broken. She traced her fingers along a deep crack in in the stone. Iluma flitted closer for inspection. The giant stone was a fluorescent yellow, it glowed with enough light that it was just visible when they neared it. It was large enough to fit more than a house in. She was amazed at its' size. She walked around it, feeling it with her hand, until she found what she was looking for. There was a deep crack in it that appeared black, stretching up the side of it in a jagged line running all the way up the side.

Teri shook her head. "I don't know how to repair this, and I don't know where any more would be unless it is harvested straight from the mines." There was a deep disappointment in her tone. "There's no way that we can make it to the mines and back on foot tonight. We would have to have a vehicle."

Iluma shook her head. "We don't have to go to the mines. The gods always know more than they tell us. I know why I'm here now. It would have either been me or possibly Traegar that could do this. I can fix it, but not the same way that she could. She could actually repair it. I can't, but I can bring out its' light, its' energy."

Teri looked at her bewildered. "Are you sure? Do you even know what this is?"

She shook her head. "I don't have to. I only have to find its' light frequency, and make it happen."

"Let's see it then," said Teri.

Iluma flew into the damaged crevice in the huge stone and reached both of her hands around the edges of the damaged part of the giant crystal and began to hum. Soon, she was glowing the same color as the stone, and the sound became louder. Soon, the stone responded with its' own yellow glow, and it became more and more bright as the humming became louder. Soon, the hum was as loud as a jet flying over them and the light was blinding to look at. Teri could only watch until the poor fairy collapsed onto the floor with the cost of her exertion. Turbines started turning, the noise roared around them, and then lights started appearing throughout the vast space. They could hear various machines whirring, clicking, and starting up all around them. Teri looked down at the fairy and gently picked her up.

"Bless you," she said, and she carried her gently as she left the room, stalling at the door to retrieve the gun from the bag that they had found earlier with her free hand.

XI: On the Run

Michael flew through the air and slammed against the wall on the far side of the stairwell before sliding down and catching his feet. The explosion was on purpose. James and Shiana would be safe now, or so he thought. Kim had flattened herself against the wall, so that she had not been thrown. The explosion did not stop the footsteps of the Mahldrusecs from coming closer. In fact, it had summoned more.

"Michael, what were you thinking?" Kim shouted. She aimed her guns at the creatures coming toward them, but she knew that they would not be enough.

"Run, Michael, we are outnumbered. Go! Go! Go!" She urged him forward as the two ascended the stairs at top speed.

They dashed into the door on the next available floor and there was another explosion, as the door was sealed. Michael panted with the exertion, quickly collecting himself as the creatures pounded on the door.

"We can't stop!" Kim shouted, staring at the inoperable door. "We've got to keep going." As she said the words, the lights suddenly came on, sparks shot from the key panel by the door and it sizzled. They stared around for a moment, looking at their surroundings, taking in where they were as Kim gained her feet more slowly. There were sounds through the doors nearby.

"Wherever we are," said Michael, "It's probably not anywhere that we want to be." They looked around at the vast space surrounding them. It was filled with bright, florescent lighting, and they were in a wide hallway painted black with silver and white accents. It almost seemed elegant. There were many doors on each side of it. All of the doors were closed.

"Wait a minute," said Kim. "She stepped forward and tried one of the handles. There was no key hole, instead there was a keypad. She put her ear to door, listening.

"We have got to get off of this floor." She whispered. "These are their homes. Those things live on this floor, I think." she said, with wide-eyes, staring at Michael

Michael looked at her, panicked. *"What do we do? How do we get out of here?"* He said telepathically.

They both jumped as they heard a banging on the exploded door behind them, and they could see a sizable dent poke into it. "There has to be a window somewhere," Kim whispered. "Come on. We've still got rope. Maybe we can use it to get to the floor that Shiana is on."

"Have you tried talking to her or James telepathically?" Michael asked, in her mind, as they ran forward.

"No, I tend to not do that while I'm trying to see what could happen next," she said aloud. Speaking telepathically at the moment would take away from her future-sight.

"Well, they're not speaking," he said.

Kim shook her head. "I can't think about that right now, Michael. Just keep running. We've got to find them. We've got to get to them. The lights are on now. We could risk an elevator, but we might get trapped in it with those things." They turned a corner. There were more doors.

"At the end of the corridor, turn left. I see it already. There's an elevator. We can get in it. There shouldn't be any Mahldrusecs...if we can get there in time.

Suddenly, they heard a sound from somewhere behind them. A door opened and they could hear a creature emerging. There was a loud roar as it spotted them.

"Hey," it shouted. "Get back here!"

"Just go!" said Michael. *"There's no one in the elevator, right?"*

"Not yet," said Kim.

They rounded the corner and Kim hit the button, then drew her weapon. Before the elevator could ding, the creature had found them.

"Use your guns first, Michael!" Kim shouted. "If you blow up that elevator, all we have is the rope!"

Michael was charged at full-speed by the creature and pinned against the wall, its' claws wrapped around his neck.

Kim aimed a straight shot at the creature's head. The bullets pierced, and there was a sizzling sound. The creature looked at her, a mix of some animal, rotting human flesh, and mechanical demon.

There was an earsplitting roar, and they could hear more doors opening in the hallway.

The creature dropped Michael and lunged at her. There were sounds throughout the hallway as other creatures came to investigate the gunshots. She dodged as Michael's gun clicked and as the bullet hit the creature's leg, there was a louder crackling sound. The creature fell on one leg as it let out a painful roar. The other creatures' footsteps pounded closer. Kim aimed a well-placed kick at the beast's jaws, and then quickly withdrew as Michael shot again, this time in the other leg. Kim shot at its' face immediately after. Its roar was deafening. The other creatures were just rounding the corner, displaying a multitude of weapons each when the elevator doors opened and the two selbdes slid inside and immediately hit the button for the floor that Shiana and James were on when they had been separated. Gunshots flew from their guns, repeatedly striking the mahldrusecs in the front of the group to hold the creatures off until the doors closed and they began a descent.

Kim laughed at their escape as she shook all over. A nervous sweat was pouring from her forehead, and Michael leaned against the wall, his breathing heavy.

"What are those things?" he asked with exclamation. "They're not like the regular mahldrusecs," he observed, as he rubbed his reddened neck.

Kim shook her head. "Something that I don't want to have to fight again," she said, and then the door opened. This hallway was dimly lit with pale, red light, and there was an immediate sense of foreboding as they stepped out. A blood trail led down the hallway. They were both quiet.

Michael looked at her questioningly. He didn't know where they should go. Kim looked confused for a moment, then she shook her head and motioned back towards the elevator and put a finger to her lip to let him know to be quiet. Slowly and quietly, they slid back into the elevator and Kim hit a button for the ground floor.

"What are we doing?" Michael said.

Kim shook her head. "We're not looking for them there. There are too many mahldrusecs on that hall. We'll never take them by ourselves. There is no way in hell that I'm up for that fight right now. We wouldn't survive it."

"So, where do you think they are? If they're on that hall, we have to find them."

Kim shrugged. "I don't know, but I suggest that we go back to that office that Shiana showed us and try to regroup with Teri and Iluma. We stand a better chance of survival if we come back with more numbers. We might even have Sassy come, if she can.

Michael sighed heavily, knowing that Kim was right, but wanting nothing more than to go back into that hallway if it meant finding James and Shiana. He crossed his arms, and breathed heavily with agitation as the elevator fell lower.

XII. The Split Decision

Victor walked back towards the ladder at the kial tree, not surprised to see the silhouette of Celeste waiting for him. As he walked towards her, he sighed heavily as he realized what he had to do. Despite his mood, he smiled as he approached her. She reached out to him. Her embrace was all comfort for him. He held to her, letting that warmth, her love, fill him. It was like the night that he finally had her home, when they were finally alone after all those years. They hardly spoke, just held to each other as he tried to make sense of the memories that he was gathering. It hurt him, deep in his soul. He realized then what the sky goddess had taken from them. He had been so overwhelmed, that all he could do was hold to her. Of course, eventually there was more than holding, but that first wave of pain from what she had endured, his own guilt, and the relief that she was finally home had simply been overwhelming for them both. They had been afraid to let go. This embrace felt almost the same.

"I understand," she finally said. "Some promises must be broken, and it's okay, we are both breaking them." They had made many promises, one of them being that no matter what, they would stay together. They did not want to risk being lost again, especially not to each other. Things had changed though. With the news that they had received from the moon elf, they knew that Celeste would have to go find Arik, and Victor would have to tend to his duties as the angel of justice at their castle. The hunters under his blood spell would be bound to him, seeking him out. It was too dangerous for him to be anywhere near the Scithronians, or traveling. The hunters were a threat that had to be stopped, preferably away from others, just in case things got out of hand, and justice was forced to show his full might. He had a lot to do to rebuild, as well as ending the hauntings of memories and pains still plaguing him from Celeste's past.

Victor did not let go of his wife. Despite what he had to do, letting go, leaving her, it felt like an end to everything good to him.

"I can still feel it," he admitted to her. "I still feel the burning, the torture...and the things the sky goddess did to you. I have to stop it." He swallowed hard as she pulled away, and he wrapped his hands in hers.

"I know that you are afraid that it may happen again, Victor, but at least we can see it coming this time," she held to his hands, her grip soft, but firm, "and you are right. It must end. You have a solid plan. I believe it will work. Leaving you is not any easier for me, but sometimes it is for the best, and look on the bright side, at least you will have Angelik with you. She kept me from being consumed by the darkness. Maybe she will do the same for you."

He nodded. "Maybe," he said. He could no longer hold back the tears of blood. They came from the pain that he now endlessly felt, the pain of her torture mixed with the warmth she gave him now, her endless beauty, and strength from within was more than he could stand at the moment, knowing that he didn't know when he would see her again.

"You have to come back to me this time. I know now that I am powerless without you. Please, don't let Carmina leave your side," he begged. "I trust her. I know that she'll do everything that she can, if she must, to protect you." He looked deep into her eyes.

Celeste smiled, "and who says I can't protect myself?" she said with a teasing smile.

Victor laughed slightly at her spunk. "I have no doubts about that either," he said, his own smile returning, "but where would I have been all those years ago, if not for

Slatkin?" he asked. "Keep your friends close," he said, "especially if they can fight as well as Carmina can."

Celeste smiled. "I will let her go with me. You will have Angelik, and even though she is still coming into her power, she has a great ability to pull us from darkness. She has done that for me many times." Victor nodded, and reached up to smear his tears across his face, but Celeste stopped him, and handed him the cloth that Arista had shared with her.

"Use this," she said, "Trust me."

He wiped his face and was puzzled when the cloth came away clear. Celeste smiled.

"It's from the elves. We really should learn more about them when this is all over," she said. Victor nodded in agreement.

"Well," Celeste sighed, "let us go break the news to them." Victor released his grip on her hand, and they made their way back into the underground den.

When they reached the bottom of the ladder, Victor went to find Barrett, to get his horse ready. Celeste turned to Klarissa first. The seer looked at her with no surprise in her eyes.

"You're leaving tonight," the seer said.

Celeste reached out to embrace the young woman. "Many thanks for the splendid feast," she said, as she pulled away, "but we have much to do." Klarissa nodded with understanding.

"Barrett is already preparing the horses. Your journey, I can't see it. It is shrouded in darkness. That does not bode well for you, not in these times. Though, whether it is shadow or sorrow, I cannot tell. It is a mystery for me."

Celeste listened intently, taking the words to heart. Klarissa was very gifted as a seer. Her words left the angel feeling wary.

"Thank you, Klarissa. I have faith that you will know if we need aid."

Klarrissa nodded. "We will be here, awaiting your orders, my queen."

Next, Celeste turned and walked to her sister, Alexandria, and waited until the end of her story. It was the one where she gained the scars over her eye. Fights with magic and beasts were always better with an audience, she thought. She could tell some of the Scithronians had questions at the end, but Alexandria excused herself to speak to the queen alone.

"So, you're leaving tonight?" Alexandria asked, reading her soul before Celeste could even speak. Celeste nodded.

"I'm going to miss you," she said. "Please don't make it so long next time," she said. Alexandria smiled as she quickly embraced her sister.

"It shouldn't take more than a few weeks to travel to Chimrion, gather a good-sized army, and travel back here. The traveling back here will take the longest. I think I'm the only one from Chimrion to have ever made it this far north," she said. "I'll have to make sure they are up to it before we leave, but I'm confident that they will help me...they owe me some favors anyway," she said. "You be careful," she said, "I know you owe it to this elf, but don't get lost again," she said. "Your people need you."

Celeste nodded. "I'll be careful," she said. Alexandria nodded in response. Celeste knew that was her

119

way of telling her that she loved her. As an angel of vengeance, Alexandria often had funny ways of showing her own love.

She turned and walked over to Carmina next, who waited patiently for her queen.

"Carmina, will you accompany us on our quest?" she asked.

The nephilim, who was so tall that she already had to duck under the low ceiling of the den, was more than pleased to curtsy to her queen.

"I am at your service, my queen," she said.

"To start," said Celeste, "perhaps you can summon the kraelvins. Maybe they have news of Arik."

"I will ask them, my queen," she said.

"Thank you," said Celeste.

She walked over to the bench where her daughter lay sleeping. The hardest goodbye yet. She looked at her sweet, beautiful face, felt the brightness of her soul that somehow seemed to seep out to everything around her. She slept on the bench, exhausted from the excitement of the feast and activities of the night. Celeste brushed back a golden curl from her face, and Angelik's eyes fluttered open.

Celeste felt a smile spread over her. "Hey, my sweet angel," she said. Angelik sat up drowsily, rubbing her eyes. Celeste wrapped her in the warmest embrace she could summon. The little angel's hands wrapped back around her mother, in response. Celeste held to her.

"I have to say goodbye for a little while." Angelik pulled away and she looked at her mother with her wide eyes.

"I know," she said. "It's what you have to do. I'll stay with Father," she said. Celeste nodded, knowing that the child knew and understood more than anyone gave her credit for.

"I'm going to miss you," Celeste said, "but I don't know where I'm going, and it could be dangerous for you." Angelik nodded a response.

"Yeah, I know," she said. "Anyway, I feel like I need to stay with Father," she said. "He's hurting right now." Celeste nodded and forced a smile. She felt both pride and worry. It was such a large burden for such a small child to be overwhelmed with these things, but that was the way of the world.

"I love you, Angelik," she said, "and I promise not to stay longer than I should." Angelik embraced her mother, and then they stood.

"Let us go find your father now, so that you two can be on your way." Angelik nodded as her mother led her away through the tunnels that led to the stables.

XIII. Khanhine

Saltook was the oldest of the khanhine-lupa alive, and the owner of the Howling Wolf tavern. He had left his tavern in the care of Lazaris, his future son-in-law, a capable werewolf that he had taken into his own pack. He knew that he couldn't run his business for now because he had been quested with something much more important. He was taking care of a young hunter and seeing that he made it across the island to the Wards, a tribe that could teach him how to use his newly discovered gifts. Most of the pack traveled with the young hunter now, and the wolves urged Galan forward even though exhaustion, guilt, and grief wore heavy on the young boy. He ate when they gave him food. He slept when he could, but the numbness he felt was overwhelming at times. He didn't sleep much, and when he did, he dreamed of his father, the leader of the hunters, that he had recently slain with the help of the gods that he had called upon.

Saltook closed his eyes, assured that they would be safe here for the night, though it was an alert sleep, one without much rest, but Galan was sleeping now and had been for a while.

Galan was dreaming now, he knew, yet he couldn't wake, though he tried. The demon wolf stared back at him. It was his father, twisted somehow, it wasn't the father that he remembered. The demon creature grinned an evil, wolfish grin, with the old angel's blood still dripping from his teeth. He was trying to run, but his father was chasing him. The ground was full of ashes where there should have been snow and he was sinking into them. They opened up and he fell into a pit, he could taste them in his mouth and feel them smothering his face as he descended into the ground, being buried under more ashes than he could claw away.

He awoke then gasping for air, a cold sweat had covered him. He shivered in the cold, but got up and walked away from the wolves. The night was clear and full of stars. The moon was white and high in the sky. He took a few moments to catch his breath, his teeth chattering uncontrollably. He reached into the pack at his side and pulled out his sister's stone. He wondered what she was doing now. He felt then a dread fall over him. It would be too long before he saw her again, and his mother.

He stood staring at the stone, wondering if it would ever speak to him. The Mother had said that the stones speak differently to the men than the women, but he was curious. He thought of Khanhine, the god of the hunters, and remembered calling for him just before he had killed his father. Suddenly, the stone seemed to glow in his hand. It was a foggy grayish blue glow, but it was there.

"You're a natural," he turned towards the voice. A man stood before him. He was dark-skinned and wore silver furs. A crown of antlers adorned his head. Galan didn't recognize him as any hunter he had ever met, but then he knew who he was.

"Khanhine," he said.

"Yes," the god confirmed.

There was a long silence. "I don't have all night. You summoned me, so tell me why."

"Can't you tell?" Galan asked.

Khanhine looked at him for a moment and then folded his arms. "Not with you," he replied.

"And why not?" Galan asked.

Khanhine shrugged. "I'm not sure. You are with my children, so I trust you, but I cannot understand you."

Galan looked to him. "Do you have guidance for me?" he asked. "You helped me, but I don't understand what's happening." A tear slid from the boy's eye. "I don't understand," he said.

"There is not much to it, child," he said. "You called me and so I came."

"But why?" he said. "You could have chosen not to."

Khanhine looked down at the snow, deep in thought, then he looked back at the boy, his silver eyes shining. "The things that you fought used to be my subjects. I cared for them, but Nometheog ruined them, and I reasoned that if you were against Nometheog, then I should help you."

"So, Nometheog, the god of the void, did he kill my father or did I?"

"That's not a question for me," said Khanhine. "That's one for Saigolai. I don't know. As for guidance, I teach how to hunt, to show respect for life. We must take life only to give life, but we must show respect. These men that raised you, they have no respect. They used to. The hunt is meant to sustain the life that Saigolai gives, not to take unnecessarily. They would do the bidding of Nometheog and destroy when opportunity arises. A true hunter would not kill the doe if there is no need and would set it free if he saw her trapped. If you did kill, then it was out of necessity. Sometimes that is just the way of life." He looked at Galan, piercing him with his gaze. "You look upon me and feel no fear," he observed.

"Should I?" Galan asked. "Feel fear, I mean? Because I feel nothing. Everything seems distant to me right now. I miss my mother, and I worry about my sister, and I don't understand why, but I miss my father. Not the one that

129

tried to kill me, but the other one. He hurt me and my mother, but he taught me things, too. He loved me, I think, in the only way that he knew how to...at least I think that he did, but really, the Wards, what can they really do for me?"

Khanhine shrugged. "You won't know if you don't go to them. Perhaps you will be surprised."

Galan nodded. "Okay," he said. "Can my dogs come back to me now?" he asked.

Khanhine laughed. "They will see you soon, boy."

Galan nodded. "I won't keep you any longer, then.

Khanhine vanished as soon as he had appeared and when Galan looked down at the stone, it appeared again as just a plain rock in his hand. He hurried back to the wolves then, before they realized that he had left them.

XIV. Kristiniva's Arrival

David stared into the vision around him as it suddenly faded. He felt a panic deep in his gut. He wanted to call out to Shiana, but he was afraid to say anything at all.

Finally, Amicus spoke, his hand resting on David's shoulder. "The others will go. The portal will close when Aqualon realizes what happened. They will be able to save them."

David looked around the room. "I should have gone," he said. "We should never have involved your people in this war." He was vaguely aware that he was whispering, though it felt as if he were shouting. "I stayed here to prove to you that we weren't lying. Now they have Shiana. I need to go to her. I need to know that she is alive." His voice was all panic. Suddenly, the door opened and all eyes turned to

Kristiniva, who was just arriving. Her black hair matched the night, and her eyes glimmered with starlight. Her skin was a deep purple, like the clouds that streamed over the moon. She was clothed in deep black with a crown of distant, small stars on her head. She was like a shadow of night leaking into the room.

"You're all still here," she said, mocking surprise.

"Mother!" Amicus exclaimed. "You're here!" his tone was hopeful.

She floated towards them, gliding through the room and taking her place at the table.

The look Adrianna gave her mother was knowing, cold, and as sharp as a knife.

"My wife!" Kialo motioned for her to come closer. "I see that your winter nights have become lovelier with each day. Colder, and icier, though you managed to give us the full moon, despite the cold."

She cut her eyes at her husband. "I'm not the only one responsible for the moon," she reminded him. "Luna must have her say as well."

"Ah, yes," he replied. "Good of you to let her shine tonight."

There was a rumble of thunder then that shook the entire castle. Stiff silence followed.

"So how is the warmongering going?" she asked, looking at the other gods, a cold smile forming on her lips.

Amicus walked over to her, reaching out to take her hand, but she jerked it away before he could touch her.

"Mother?" he asked.

"I will not be staying," she said, holding up her hand, as if to command his silence. "I only came to see how things were going."

"Things are falling apart," said David.

Kristiniva couldn't supress her laughter. "Of course, they are," she said, "things always do when they are not more carefully considered."

She stared at David. "Your people knew exactly what they were walking into when they left. You have only endangered the lives of the Sheans that left with them. You could have all gone to Sark, and left us a kingdom of peace. Instead, you bring war to our kind."

"You offered help," said David. "If you didn't intend to help, then why didn't you kill us to start with and save any hope that we might still have?"

She smiled. "I never offered. If it were up to me, you'd all still be in the holding cells, or held in my castle. If it were up to me, I would have protected you, kept you safe, and never offered you anything that could be confused for something so foolish as hope in a hopeless situation."

"It is not hopeless!" Adrianna exclaimed, as she stood, her voice a deep roar, as she cast away the haze that had been around her before, and materialized fully into the room.

"Oh, but it is hopeless!" Kristiniva said, as she stood, staring her daughter in the eyes. "For the Shadow has more than darkness, more than destruction. Nometheog is strong. As strong as Saigolai. I do not wish to go up against either of them...but for what it is worth, I do hope we claim a victory." She stood then and looked at David. "Of course, my castle is always open to you and your kind, should you need protection." She turned then and made her way towards the door, a blast of wind blowing the doors open as she glided out.

Kialo looked at David. "I am sorry for my wife's stormy mood. She is fearful, as we all are."

Amicus looked at his father. "Fearful? Is that what you think she is?" he asked. "I didn't see fear when I looked at her. I saw control. She is not herself."

Kialo shrugged. "I can't say that any of us would be ourselves after the ordeal that she has recently been through. It will take time for her to find her sunny skies again." Amicus turned to his sister, who was venting steam from herself. The tendrils were gone, and she seemed more solid than she had before, her trident shining in her hand.

"Perhaps one of us should go check on her," the sea goddess said, glaring at her brother.

"I will go," he said. Then he turned to David. "Please, don't give up hope. Our champions are worthy of this task," he said, looking at David. "We will see them all back, or I shall go myself, if need be. I will not fear any other god, especially one that cannot gain his own physical form." He turned then to leave.

Adrianna looked at David. "We can bring the others to you, for you will need them. They are your foundation right now. I know what you must be feeling. We will see that she is returned to you. As for your brother I make no such promises. I will see Nometheog ended, even if your brother must end with him. Though, perhaps there is hope with our champions. Stay alert! She may come back to you at any moment."

The sea goddess turned to the elves that guarded the door. "Go retrieve the others," she said. They bowed to her and left through the double doors.

David was taking deep breaths, reminding himself that there was still hope. Shiana could still be alive and she was with James, which was the best of luck. If she were hurt, then he could heal her. He closed his eyes, trying to remember the beach she often thought of to help him get lost, it required a great deal of concentration, memory, and meditation to calm himself in the fantasy without her there to guide him, but soon, he was there, and even if the gods spoke to him, he wouldn't hear them, only her, if she would come to him. To him, it was real, and he was there. Perhaps the gods could see it too. He didn't really care who is was enveloping at the moment.

It was dark, though, and nothing he did could bring the sun to the sky. It was vast and full of stars. Clouds swept over the moon and a storm lay on the horizon across the water. Perhaps he was inadvertently connecting with the sky goddess. He shrugged and sat down next to the black water lapping over silver sand.   The water was warm, and comforting, steady in its' rolling waves. He reached out to her with everything that he had.

"Shiana!" There was no answer. "Shiana! Answer me!" He turned behind him, but there was nothing but silver sand as far as he could see.

Aqualon sat listening to the shell and staring ahead, as if listening or watching something so interesting that he could not break away. Sassy had been pacing every now and then, but then she would sometimes stop and stare uneasily at the darkness around her. So far, the night had been silent, but suddenly, Aqualon made a quick motion with his hand and the portal dissolved.

"What is it?" Sassy asked, turning to him.

Traegar suddenly looked as if she were breathing again and she turned slowly to face them.

"Shiana," said Aqualon, "I think she may have been captured. Her thoughts were suddenly stopped. I think she was hit from behind. There was an explosion." He looked at the panicked look on Sassy's face. "And things are much worse in Shea." He grabbed the shell. "I have a feeling that you won't find the Shadow in the city. Its' creatures, maybe, but not the god of void. Go, your friends need you," he said. "I'll stay here, just in case I'm wrong. If you're not back by tomorrow, I'll go after you."

Sassy nodded.

Aqualon looked at Treagar. "Do you think you can carry her with you?"

Treagar nodded. Aqualon looked at Sassy. "Don't forget to breathe," he said. Treagar smiled and wrapped her arms around the young girl as if she were about to hug her, or possibly pick her up, but then suddenly, they both appeared to be one giant stone as Treagar was keeping Sassy hidden inside of her. The stone seemed to disappear into the sand beneath Aqualon's feet and he smiled, wondering what Sassy would think of moving beneath the dirt like a troll.

XV. Shekley Without the Shadow

Xandra unhooked the IV when Shekley's color came back to him. He slept still, and she let him. While he was sleeping, she prepared his food. It was soup. She wasn't sure when he had eaten last, and she thought it best if he started on liquids first. When he finally woke up, she was laying on the bed with him. The soup had been left on the table beside of him. He smiled when he saw her, but he didn't speak. She took his hand in hers. It was still wrapped in bandages from when he had been burned by the Shadow.

"How are you feeling?" she asked. "Can you sit up? I have made some soup if you are hungry."

Slowly, Shekley raised himself into a sitting position. "I need my armor," he said, grabbing his chest to stifle pain.

"Not yet," said Xandra, sitting up and getting off of the bed to stand with quick, fluid motion. "You need to walk on your own. You need your own strength while he's not inside of you."

Shekley nodded his submission, but didn't want to say it out loud. Xandra was right. He had become too dependent on the armor. The shadow had weighed him down, stolen his strength, and left him next to death. He needed to get strong enough to fight it again. Next time, he may not have life in him when it left, and then he would just be left to Darkhan. He didn't want to think about that. She was always right, and he was so glad that she was here to be a voice of reason for him.

She walked over to the table and handed him the bowl. He ate, his hands and arms shaking slightly as he put the spoon to his mouth. Every moment of this was difficult, but Xandra did not let him give up.

"I hope it stays gone long enough for you to walk," she said. "Maybe we can walk away from here."

Shekley laughed at the absurdity, causing a pain in his chest, he wheezed in a breath. Then he looked at her, seriously, his smile fading. "Don't do that to me," he said. "I need more than a dream to get me out of here."

"Okay," she said. She was quiet then. She stood and walked over to the curtained window and pulled the curtains aside. She left him to eat, the bowl shaking in his hands, as soup spilled onto the blankets. She looked out over the night which was slowly disappearing into dawn. "We are somewhere new. Do you know what's out there, past the gate? Do you even remember going out there with me?"

Shekley shook his head. "I don't remember anything," he said, "you know that."

She nodded. "Well, I remember. There's a wilderness out there. Trees, snow, rivers. Maybe there's something else also. I want you to walk out there with me one day. Just you, and I want you to remember what you see."

Shekley looked down at his soup. "You think I wouldn't like that?" he said, his voice was quiet, a whisper. For a long time Xandra just stared out the window, perhaps wishing for some dream-like future, perhaps a reality that was completely different, and perhaps she wished for non-existence for them both.

Later, Shekley stared down at his once great city from atop the roof of the highest tower of the citadel. A morning sky, blue and bright with sunlight revealed things that he had not seen while he was shadowed. What once had been his kingdom lay broken beneath him. His great metal city, an impenetrable fortress of quiet and order had been re-formed to fit the desires of the Shadow. All of its greatness, its beauty, forged and beaten into a nightmare that he had never meant to sculpt. He knew this now. He could see it plain now. He could see it because the veil of the Shadow had been lifted from his eyes. He could barely stand on his own. Xandra had made him attempt it several times. He could stand, but he couldn't walk yet. After hours of begging, she had helped him into his robotic armor which assisted his every movement, controlled by a chip implanted in his head. He had made it years ago to help him defeat his brother. It was one thing that had somewhat put them on equal footing. He promised her that he would try again later. For now, he was glad to have steady feet and the shaky movement had stopped. Things were calmer, less painful now.

The power of the darkness had used him and worn him down until he was a pathetic waste of a human body. He knew this, but he did not know how to help himself. Without Xandra looking out for him, he doubted if he would still exist at all. Both body and soul would have shriveled up and wasted away. She was the only one that cared for him when the Shadow was gone. He had been barely able to breathe at the time, much less eat or drink. The Shadow had been gone from him for many days. Perhaps forever. Shekley thought that it was more probable that it was biding its time. It would be back. He knew and understood that the Shadow had already undone him. It made a promise to him years ago. It had promised to release the goddess. It had lied. He knew this now, but he was too weak to resist its allure whenever it did come back. He wanted now for his brother to come. Perhaps for the first time in his whole life, he was able to wish without interference from someone else in his thoughts. He was a man now. No longer a boy. Perhaps if

David were here to broadcast his thoughts, the world could be remade. He could build a new life...but like the Shadow, his brother had left him and there was no hint of when or if he would ever be back. There were only fragments of memories lingering from a long-ago, displaced childhood.

Xandra was next to him again. Shekley realized that he desired something more, some spark of life. Xandra's words were stuck in his head. Could he just walk away? He doubted it, but suddenly, there was a hope. There had been only the darkness for so long. Truth be told, he feared the monsters prowling the halls of the citadel, the ones that he had helped create. The Shadow instructed them, not him. He was glad that Xandra had locked him away in his room on the highest floor of the citadel.

"Xandra," his own voice sounded low and weak without the Shadow. He reached a hand out to hers. "Do you think there's a chance he will come for me?"

"The Shadow always comes back," she said.

"No. I meant David. Do you think he'll search for me again?"

She shrugged. "I don't know." Shekley nodded, he had spoken to her, but he didn't have it in him to look at her. They both stared ahead, seemingly towards the gate, but really, they stared past the gate, into the mountains of wilderness in the distance and the ocean beyond.

"Do you still love me?" he asked, still looking ahead of him.

She nodded. "When the Shadow is gone, I do."

The words made Shekley frown.

"Me too," he said as they gazed into the cold and distant stars of the alien world around them, wishing, hoping, and dreaming. Shekley did not know how long they stood there, but he didn't want the moment to end. But all good things come to an end, and their moment was soon broken

by sudden lights and the sounds of alarms blaring rudely all

around as various machines turned on throughout the city.

XVI: The Kraelvins

Carmina grabbed her pack and ascended the ladder into the cold, Sarkian air. Arista was close behind her, while Celeste stayed inside, saying her goodbyes.

"You may not want to come too close. They are shy and I am usually alone," the nephilim said.

"Of course," Arista replied as she backed away to stand near the closest tree. Carmina pulled thick candles out of her pack and placed them in a circle around her, then lit them each as she knelt down, there was one for each of the birds who could help her. Not all of them always answered. The kraelvins were always busy, spying on all the lands, but she hoped at least one of them would come. She sat in the circle waiting patiently for her friends. Three of them came, first circling, then swooping out of the darkness. They were large, sleek, black-feathered birds with blue eyes. They circled around the candles for a moment, then they landed within the circle. Carmina reached out and stroked their feathers.

"Hello, my helpful friends. What news do you bring tonight of the lost elf prince?"

They walked around in circles and seemed to do some sort of dance and then one of them spoke with a deep and croaky voice:

We come, we come with news

The elf prince is dark and bruised.

Blood runs deep in darkest roots

Beneath the tree he lies under its shoots.

The second bird then spoke:

Through the deepest of the dark

He has just now re-entered Sark

He is alone and not himself

Luna's light can't reach the elf

Then the third said his lines:

He is torn, forgotten, lost

He waits now in the frost

Near the barren lands he lies

Watching for Luna in the skies.

Then they all spoke at once:

The goddess hunts this night,

Pain and darkness now fight,

They seek him out to take away

So, the goddess' plans won't stray.

Carmina reached into her pack and gave the birds snacks of dried berries and nuts.

"Thank you, my friends," she said. She stroked their sleek feathers and watched them eat their meal. When they had gotten their fill, the birds flapped their large wings and flew off into the darkness. The nephilim snuffed out the candles and put them back into her pack, then turned to the elf princess. She would have to try to explain the rhyme. The angels did not understand the language of the birds and she was not sure if the elf did, but then Arista surprised her.

"Near the barren lands," she said. "I can open a portal to take us there."

Carmina looked to the ladder where the others were now emerging.

"Have you discovered anything?" Celeste asked, walking forward.

"He needs help. It sounds like he is in a lot of pain. He has escaped the cave but he is not himself. They said he's beneath a tree," Carmina responded.

Arista nodded. "Yes, I have seen it in their minds. Near the barren lands. I know the tree. It is ancient and tall. I know where to go now. Thank you," she said to the nephilim. Carmina curtsied.

They turned then as Barrett came from the forest, leading their horses. Alexandria gave quick hugs to Celeste, Victor, and Angelik, then bowed to Arista and Carmina. "May you find peace and hope until we meet again," she said, then she mounted her unicorn, Vortex. "I have a lot of ground to cover," she said. She waved and then was quickly off to gain allies in Chimrion.

Celeste embraced her daughter next, who clung to her mother in a deep embrace. "Don't stay gone too long," she said.

Celeste pulled away, looking her daughter deep in the eyes, "I won't. I promise, I will be back as soon as I can." They smiled, and then Victor lifted the young angel onto his horse, Dexon. Then he turned to Celeste, and they held each other again, then they broke their embrace, nodding to each other, knowing already what the other was feeling. It was a nod of understanding and determination that they would see each other soon.

He mounted Dexon, and Angelik waved back to the three women who stood watching them ride away as Victor kicked the horse into a gallop. He did not look back. Carmina reached out to Celeste.

"We must go now," she said, pulling her away from the emotional goodbye. "Arik is in danger. I think it's hunters."

Celeste turned to Barrett, who had been standing by with the rest of the horses. She reached out to hug him, remembering him from his childhood. A small boy who was always ready to fight the other children when he saw them do something wrong. "Thank you, Barrett, and please stay safe." He beamed with pride.

"I am always here to serve you, my queen," he said, as he handed over the reins to her mare.

Celeste smiled at him, and the three women mounted their horses, and were soon traveling through a portal, woven by Arista.

Arista was the first off of her horse, a troubled look crossing her face as she looked at the tracks in the snow, a mix of footprints, horse tracks, blood, and something that had been pulled behind someone. She breathed heavily, and clutched the hilt of the sword hanging at her side.

"We're too late," she said. Celeste ran forward, up the slope of the mountain and gazed out to the barren lands beyond the cliffs. A pale, red dawn was shining pink over the land below. Carmina and Arista followed her and they gazed down. No words were needed. They could see the two horses in the distance, making their way to the black fortress beyond as the sky began to lighten with the approaching dawn.

"I'm going after him," said Arista.

"Wait," said Celeste as she turned to Arista. "We will all go," she said. "If my promise takes me there, then so be it."

Arista nodded then turned back towards the tree. The smell of freshly chopped wood was heavy in the air. She walked forward, and put her hand to the tree. The others looked on. The elf wept, her hands were shaking and glowing as she connected with the tree. She fell into a deep sadness as she wept, listening to the tree as it told her what it knew of her brother and the reasons for its scarred bark.

When she pulled away, she looked up to its old, wide branches. "Thank you," she said. She walked over to where it had been hacked and pulled a vial of what looked like water from her pocket and let two drops fall onto the wood.

"Maybe it will help," she said to the tree.

Then she turned to the others. Her face was set in anger and defiance. "I know now what it means to lose the moon," she said. She turned then to the moon, large and white, but not quite full yet.

"Luna," she whispered, "Is there nothing you can do?" she asked. Tears filled her eyes.

"He is not himself," she said to the others, "because Kristiniva took the moon from him. Do not expect him to be the same. He is dark now, and I do not know what we can do. Even though the moon shines bright in the sky tonight, he can't even see it. He can't feel her love. There is nothing to give him vitality now."

Celeste shook her head. "If Victor doesn't beat me to it, I will end the goddess myself," she said.

"Let's go," said Arista, her face set in determination. "We have to get to him before they can do any more harm to him."

They mounted the horses and followed the tracks of the hunters into the barren lands.

XVII. Shekley's Message

James awoke with a splitting headache. All was dark around him, and he felt disoriented. He couldn't remember where he was. There was the memory of the door slamming, the explosion, and then he remembered that he had been hit in the back of the head. He tried to sit up, but found that his hands had been bound. Metal restraints held him down. He shivered in cold and fear. His coat and gear were all gone. He had been stripped to just his shirt and pants, which was not enough to keep him warm in this cold place. He glanced around the room but he couldn't see anyone else, only faint glowing lights here and there. There was a humming of electrical equipment around him, but no other sound. He reached out for the others with his mind to try to grasp some hope in the situation, but a headache of blinding pain was the only answer he could get and then he heard a voice. It laughed at him. It was the same voice that he had heard back in the medical room.

"I'm prepared for that. You didn't think that I could capture you without some degree of protection, did you?"

James stayed silent.

"No, Nometheog prepared me. I knew you would come...well, some of you at least. I did hope that it would be David. That's the one that my god truly wants. He's the trophy, but you'll do nicely."

James could feel the man's eyes on him, though he still couldn't see where the man was. "I've already taken your blood...the things that I can do with blood..." the man laughed. "Nometheog doesn't limit me. Here, I can mostly do as I wish. I'm starting with the blood, but I might make my way to other things.

Then he appeared out of the darkness, a hooded figure standing over him. His hood was all black, and he stared down at James with a robotic eye, his face was mostly hidden, but the glow from his eye was just enough to make out faint features. It was an all-black eye except for the iris, which glowed red. He grabbed James' arm with his hand, gloved with black, leather gloves.

James let out a noise of fear and protest, then the man pierced him with a needle. There was a cold, stinging sensation. It spread through him quickly. He could feel it tracing through his body like ice.

"Yes, the blood will do for now, but then a hair perhaps...maybe flesh. Even a bone...but I await orders and Shekley's girl doesn't like me, so we shall see what I do with you. If she doesn't need you, then I will not have boundaries.

James stayed quiet, and in his own thoughts. He couldn't read this man's thoughts, or reach out to his friends.

He couldn't even heal himself. He felt weak and cold, but mostly he was afraid. He knew the darkness of the Shadow and what it had done to Shekley. He feared now what would happen to him. The Shadow had his blood, but he did not know to what end he would use it. He tried to stay awake, but he felt drugged and heavy. It was hard to keep his eyes open and soon he was sleeping, despite his every effort to stay awake.

Darkhan smiled as he pulled out a spell book and flipped through the pages. There were still some he had not tried in here.

Shiana awoke to a headache and pain all over, she felt drained. She sat up slowly. She was in a dimly lit room, lying on a metal operating table. Xandra stood across the room, blocking the doorway, staring through her black hair with her lighted blue eye, surrounded by silver metal. Her weapons were hidden and she just stared back at Shiana with her arms folded.

They locked gazes for a moment. Shiana couldn't read her mind. If she tried, she felt pain throughout her body. She winced as a nauseous feeling overwhelmed her.

"We've fixed your intrusions," Xandra said.

Shiana fell back against the cold, metal table. "Where is James?" she asked.

"Where is David?" Xandra retorted.

"He didn't come," said Shiana.

Xandra crossed the room and reached out, pulling the selbdes close to her, and she whispered. "The Shadow is gone at the moment. I need you," she said. Shiana screamed as Xandra grabbed her arm and pulled her from the table. The mahldrusec laughed.

"That's good," she said. "They have to think I'm hurting you." Shiana had not been pretending. The force that Xandra was putting on her arm was leaving a bruise. There was nothing that she could do but let the mahldrusec lead her forward. They stopped at an elevator and Xandra thrust Shiana into it before stepping inside. They began an ascent.

"The elevators!" exclaimed Shiana in excitement. She hoped it meant that Teri and Iluma had been successful.

Xandra looked at her, puzzled. "I'm taking you to Shekley."

Shiana looked at her in fear.

Xandra did not speak. When the doors opened, she grabbed Shiana, pulling her along a hall and then they slipped through a door. When it closed, she thrust the selbdes on the floor. Shiana fell face first onto the floor, but as she rolled over to collect herself, she stopped. She was terrified to see Shekley staring down at her, but only for a moment. The man that stared back at her was not the cruel and evil man that she had known in previous years.

"Shekley?" she asked.

He nodded. "Where is David?" he asked. He sounded weary, and his voice was dry.

"He didn't come here," she said. "He's only here in thought," she said, pointing to her own head.

Shekley turned to Xandra. "Take it off," he said.

"But Shekley," Xandra began.

"It's okay, Xandra. I need to do this before the Shadow returns."

Xandra knelt down behind the selbdes and Shiana felt something being ripped off the back of her head, she let out a scream of pain.

"Find him," Shekley demanded. There was an urgency in his voice that he had not used before. It was close to desperation.

Shiana concentrated. She let her mind wander beyond the city. She found the elf, waited for him to open the portal again, and then stretched her thoughts beyond the portal.

"Shiana!" she heard the comforting sound of David's voice. *"Oh, thank God you're okay! What happened?"*

"Can you see this?" she asked him. *"Can you see where I am and who I'm with?"*

It took him a moment, and then he replied. *"Yes."*

Shiana looked up to Shekley. "He can see you," she said.

Shekley looked back at her, and closed his eyes, trying to remember what his brother looked like. So many of his memories were dark, but if he tried hard enough, he could see him as if through a gray smoke. He opened his eyes and looked at the woman kneeling before him, imagining his brother there.

"The Shadow is gone at the moment. I don't know where it is. I don't know when it will be back. It could be any time. It has been coming and going for some weeks now." He paused, deep in thought. "It wants you. It doesn't want you dead. It wants you all alive, but most especially, you. You have a purpose for it. You will make it stronger." He paused, trying to make sense of the jumbled thoughts in his head.

"I can't leave, because it will find me no matter where I go. It tricked me, David, and I see that now. It took my goddess and it will never give her back. It killed her.

This city was supposed to be a thing of beauty, but it used me to craft a nightmare. I see it clearly now because the Shadow has left me for now. It is enslaving the people of this new land, and turning them into new terrors. There's another man helping him. His name is Darkhan, and he is powerful. He has sorcery, and power over the souls of men. I am afraid of what will happen to me if I die. I feel like you are the only one that can help me now, but I don't know what to tell you. Don't come into the city. Don't risk your life for mine. Mine has already been wasted," he sighed heavily, not sure if his jumbled thoughts even made sense to anyone else.

"I think I just wanted to talk. To tell you that I'm sorry, and to say goodbye. Just let me go. I can't escape, and you won't survive if you come here. These new creatures were made with my craft and Darkhan's sorcery. Together, we have created something stronger, darker, and more horrible than anything I could have imagined on my own. Just go home. I'm not there anymore. I can't harm you if you stay away." He motioned for Xandra to return the piece to the back of Shiana's head and before the selbdes knew what had happened, David was far away again, and Shiana was staring back at a weak and powerless man, held up only with his armor.

"Take her out of the city," he said to Xandra. "If anyone asks, just tell them you're going to bury her alive. Take her far away and release her."

"Wait!" protested Shiana. "What about my friends?"

Shekley shrugged. "I don't think I can save you all."

Shiana shook her head. "No! Wait!" she screamed as Xandra pulled her forward and down the hall. "No, no, no! I can't leave without them."

Xandra lifted her up by her collar and stared at her as soon as they were out of earshot of Shekley. "I have to do what he says. I only know where one of them is, but he's with Darkhan, and I don't know if I can save him or not. Luckily, it's on our way out. Darkhan is full of evil, even when the Shadow is gone. It may already be too late."

"We have to try," said Shiana.

Xandra dropped her then onto the floor then started dragging her again. "It's okay to struggle," she said. I have to convince them," she said.

Shekley put his face in palms, rubbing his eyes. He wanted sleep now, but there was to be none. He was startled when he heard the knock at the door. He reluctantly opened it. a creature stood there, gazing at him with fear.

"The goddess Vishka summons you, in secrecy. Come, or fear her wrath." Shekley sighed deeply and reached for his helmet.

"Let's go, then," he said.

XVIII. The Special Creation

Arik had been sleeping, but he was vaguely aware of someone trying to awaken him. Then again, it could be the roots of the tree twisting him, tossing him, throwing him into the light. He tried to open his eyes, but his fatigue was too heavy, and there was a burning on his skin like hot coals where the goddess had scraped her claws into his back. He was aware of a nauseous feeling, maybe it was his hunger coming back to him. However, it was more like a dizzying feeling, like he was spinning, or moving some way that was unnatural to him. He could distantly hear voices, but his exhaustion was so severe that his sleep would not allow him to properly wake. There were deep, growling voices. His dreams imagined them as animals.

"Is this it? This pitiful thing?" the first asked. Somehow, the voice was far away, but so loud it gave him a headache.

"Check for her marks! If he has the marks, then it's him," replied the second.

There was more unnatural movement, and pains returning that had been warded off with his rest beneath the tree. The burning on his back intensified where the goddess had clawed him.

"It's definitely him. Her mark couldn't be clearer."

"Well, then, get him in here." Suddenly, there was a cool comfort. The pain on his back fled from him, and he breathed clearly again, realizing that he had been holding his breath, the burning pain had been so intense. He wasn't sure what blocked it now, but his dreams made him feel a cool stream, far away from the any light. He moved in it as the currents carried him away. It was a steady rhythm, but the stream was rocky and rough and he floated in it until the dreams became absolute again, and he dreamed memories from his life.

The creatures pulled the black sack behind them. Vishka had spoken to them and they did as she said, their brands burning with new pain until the task was complete. They came to her now, victorious in their hunt. They did not see her, but her voice spoke.

"Let's see him. For all I know, you have brought me the carcass of a slain animal. I need to know that it is him." The hunters quickly undid the ties on the sack and pulled the cursed elf out, laying him on the floor. Suddenly, the walls seemed to drip with blood, though it was just an illusion.

"Bring me Shekley!" she demanded. "I have a task for him."

"He answers to Nometheog, though," the first said.

Suddenly, a spike of black metal erupted from the ground and impaled him. He roared in pain, still alive, but unable to move.

"Not a word to Darkhan. I only need Shekley," she commanded the other in her deep growl. "Bring him to me now."

The second creature nodded a head of ram's horns and quickly fled to do as he was told.

When Arik awoke, he couldn't move, but he was sure that he was awake now. His dreams were all wasted for the moment. Through effort, he turned his head. He could see clearly in the darkness around him. A man lay on a table next to his, but across the room from him. He wasn't sure where he was or how he had gotten here. There was no way to speak to the man, but the man was definitely alive. He could see his chest rising and falling in sleep.

Arik knew he did not even have the strength to sit up, but he still tried, only to find that his hands and feet were bound in chains. He tried to feel his pain again, his broken bones, but he couldn't. There was a new pain there. It was icy, bone deep, but it was not the same as it had been before.

Then lights suddenly lit up the room. Arik closed his eyes to the brightness. Someone walked forward. He squinted up as a shadow passed over him. There was a man staring down at him. He didn't know the man. He wore a helmet on his head. He wore strange, black armor and a mask hid most of his face, but his eyes were clear, sparkling blue, but they were cold and lonely.

"He's still awake. Shall I proceed?"

"Is there a doubt?" Arik recognized the voice of the goddess that had freed him.

"Of course not," the man replied. "I can do it, but I will need time...and Xandra. I need her to assist me."

"No," the goddess spoke, "I will assist you. Xandra is keeping Darkhan from disturbing you. He will only try to change things, but you know that you are capable without either of them. Do this for me, and I will reward you."

At her words, Shekley hesitated. He knew that Xandra had not yet had time to get Shiana out of the city, but he must not inquire further. He was confident that Xandra could handle herself. "I've been promised many rewards but I've received nothing."

"My promises are different from Nometheog's. Remember, it's him that I am against. His void is stifling to me. Clearly, you feel the same. Just be creative." Arik could hear the cold delight in her voice. "This one is different from the others, and you must be careful. He must not die. If he does, then Darkhan will get a chance, and neither of us want that, so take all the time you need."

Arik was beginning to feel his heart racing, but could tell that the man was hesitant.

"I don't know that he can survive. It's a lot of blood loss, even with freezing him. It's a lot of pain. I can't imagine doing that to someone…without something to dull the pain…I mean, I have done it… it wasn't me really. Well it was, but I didn't do it willingly, I mean."

"So, do it unwillingly!" Her voice was sharp and impatient. Shekley doubled over in sudden pain.

"Okay!" he shouted, desperation crackling in his voice. "I can do it!"

He inhaled a deep breath as he recovered, the pain suddenly passing as quickly as it had come. He looked down at Arik and spoke seriously, almost sympathetically. "Sleep if you can. Just pretend it's a dream."

Arik was afraid then. There was no way to scream, and no way to fight. He shook his head and pushed as hard as he could will himself to free himself from the restraints. Some part of him hoped the man could reason with the goddess, but he knew then that he couldn't. No one could. He inhaled a breath, and then the sounds started, various unknown machines coming to life buzzing and whirring around him. His breathing was fast, while he felt the panic in his tears. He wasn't sure what the sounds were that he was hearing, and he closed his eyes against the lights now shining over him, that and the fear. He couldn't look. He understood where he was now. He was in Trost. This was Shekley and he was turning Arik into one of the things that he had vowed to fight. It was his instinct to fight, and he tried, but there was nothing that he could do except endure. Sometime, after the fear, and the pain, every kind of pain that he could imagine, and then some, the goddess hovered above him.

"I make it, I can take it away, too," she said. She placed a hand over his eyes. "Feel nothing for now. Go back to your dreams. Your struggle makes it difficult for him."

Arik felt his eyes rolling back in his head and then the pain seemed far away as he dreamed yet again. He was floating in the stars, looking for Luna, but the moon was not to be found. His dream just let him numbly travel the cosmos, alone, cold, but surrounded by a peaceful quiet.

Shekley was hesitant and nervous at every new move. The goddess had warned him that he couldn't mess this up. She told him that she would distract Nometheog, if and when he decided to return, but Shekley knew that the chances of either of them knowing was slim. Nometheog did not give warnings. He just carefully crept into place.

He couldn't remember when he had done this willingly before, just the once, many years ago. It was mostly theory, but obviously, it had worked. All he had to do to gain his confidence was to think of Xandra. She was his creation. Sure, the Shadow could command his will to Shekley to control Xandra, but ultimately the Shadow could not control her. How much better would this one be, without the Shadow's interference at all. It would be something new and even better than Xandra. He promised himself that he would be careful. This one couldn't die.

Darkhan had more than enough opportunities to play with the other bodies, but this one was his. This one would be independent. Vishka would see to that. This was one that the Shadow could not touch and even Shekley was not granted access to control. He feared this goddess, and he dared not defy her. But there was also a great admiration for her, so he did as he was told.

He told himself to concentrate on the hands and feet. They had been broken by her, and they were as much of hers as the marks from her claws on his back...Shekley had a plan for those also. He thought the goddess would appreciate it. He kept his hands steady as he worked more quickly with what blood remained now frozen in the body. It was the only way to keep this creature alive. Otherwise, the loss of blood would be too great. The metal seemed to work for him like nothing else, like it was an extension of his own thoughts, and soon he was lost in the mechanics. The body lying in front of him was nothing more than another machine, one that could be altered to function as something better, more grand, immortal, and essentially beautiful when he was finally done. Shekley looked down at the new thing lying beneath him, and felt a sense of pride. He smiled with satisfaction.

The goddess took his hand, the one that had been bandaged for months now, and carefully she unraveled the bandage and pulled it away. The deep burn was gone. There was no sign there to show that he had even ever had a burn and no pain to remind him.

"You have done well," she said, staring down at Arik in admiration. "Now, if secrets can be kept, we shall be free." She looked down at the dark elf, now finished, remade. She smiled.

"He is perfection," she said, "a lovely perfection."

Shekley couldn't help but smile at his own genius.

Then Vishka's voice growled again, "We must get him away from here, and quickly. Darkhan will be coming soon, and possibly Nometheog. How long before he awakens?"

"His blood is still thawing. It will take hours." responded Shekley.

The goddess growled. "We don't have hours. I will wake him myself, if I must. Leave us now."

Shekley nodded, and turned quickly away to leave, then the goddess fully materialized and reached out to her new and exciting fascination.

XIX. The Quinlans

Galan couldn't fall asleep, but the wolves soon woke and hastened him away. They traveled as they usually did, pressing onward through more snow, passing more trees, eating when they could, and resting when they needed to, but tonight was different. There was a new feeling in the air. Saltook stayed close by Galan's side, taking the form of the old man at the tavern.

"Are we close?" asked Galan.

Saltook shook his head and placed a finger over his own mouth to quiet the boy, then he whispered, "No, we are still far away. There is a way yet to travel, but something stirs in the trees," he whispered.

"What?" asked Galan.

Saltook shook his head. "I can't tell, but it smells of blood. Blood, metal, and decay."

Galan's eyes widened. "Like Volkhan and Haz," he whispered low.

Saltook nodded. "Do not let your guard down, and keep your weapons close. I will protect you."

Galan hoped that whatever was out there, that it was not his father somehow re-made. He did not think that he had it in him to fight him again. His wounds were still new and painful, but he clutched his bow and strung an arrow, despite the pain of burns on his hands, then he thought that if he had done it once, he could do it again. They walked forward cautiously, as Galan suddenly became more aware of where and how he stepped, then he gasped as he spotted it before them. Wind rattled through the bars of the cage as it swung from a tree, raking against a tree limb. A woman lay inside, dead, and decaying. Old blood dried to her wounds of which Galan could only guess the origins. Saltook wept then as he looked up.

Galan placed a hand on the old man's shoulder. "She was one of yours?" he asked. Saltook was too overwhelmed to speak but Basilla, Saltook's daughter, came up and spoke with tears in her own eyes, "That is my cousin. It is Saltook's niece. She's been missing for weeks."

Galan swallowed hard. He knew several people that were capable of doing this.

"I'm sorry," he said. "I will help you cut her down." He placed his bow on his back and stowed his arrow then he started climbing the tree. Even with his injuries, he climbed the tree with ease.

"Reach up and grab it," he said, after steadying himself on the tree branch. "Can you reach?" he asked, peering down at the people below him.

"I can do it," one of the taller men among them replied. He reached up, grabbing hold to the bottom of the cage with ease and it was slowly lowered down to him as Galan cut the rope.

"All the angels in the land, and there never seems to be enough of them to stop the evil," he said, as an observation. He made his way back down the tree, feeling pain in his wounds as he did so.

The girl was pulled from the cage, as many of them wept by her. Some of them mourned in wolf form, and others in human. Basilla reached out to grab a pendant from the girl's neck, and placed it in Saltook's hand.

"We need to take her body back to her mother," said Saltook. "She should have a proper ceremony."

The wolves mourned over the woman's body, and Galan leaned against the tree, solemnly contemplating their actions. Did this mean that they would abandon their mission to take him to the Wards? A large part of him hoped so. He would go find his own dogs and maybe go back to visit his mother, maybe go to the castle, where the angel had promised that he would be looked after. He wasn't sure really, but he liked the thought of doing whatever he wanted. Suddenly, he turned to stare into the trees. There was some feeling in his gut that told him they were in danger. He turned back to the wolves.

"Hide," he said. "Now!" he urged. "There's something else out there. I heard it!"

Saltook came to his side quickly, in wolf form. Galan peered through the trees, but he couldn't see anything. Suddenly, one of the wolves barked a scream of pain. It was hopping in the snow, the others running to help it. It growled then, staring into the trees before falling on the ground, its fur standing on end, turning black as black veining started appearing on its skin. Galan could only watch in horror, but then he heard the buzzing, and he turned to the sound, immediately recognizing Malik, though he was completely different. Like his father had been different. Metal veining traced its way around his skin and his eyes were black, even the whites. The buzzing was coming from his throat and when he spoke, the buzzing made his words shake.

"Galan," he said, "your father was looking for you. I see that he failed."

Galan could only stare back, the wounds of killing his father were too new, both on his body and in his soul.

"Did that sweet-smelling sister of yours get what was coming to her yet? I found a spot of her blood back near the cabin. It was just enough to excite me, and make me want more." The creature moved forward awkwardly. Galan realized that it was not walking on legs, but wings were propelling it forward. He was flying just high enough that his feet were off of the ground.

Galan felt frozen. He wasn't sure if he could fight another creature like his father, not with his burned hands and punctured shoulder. Even his words felt frozen, because he knew that if he spoke at that moment, then he would have to fight.

The creature stepped closer, and Galan realized he had a swollen, red belly poking out of his coat. The skin was thin and veined. He could see the newly devoured blood swirling underneath.

He looked at the creature in disgust.

"How about your mother?" it taunted. "Did Volkhan at least get a taste of her?" He licked his lips, which had somehow become pointed and thin.

"Turn around and go back to wherever you came from, you sick creature!" Galan said. "If you don't, then I will summon a god to smite you down where you stand."

The buzzing of laughter from Malik's throat reverberated through the trees. "He was supposed to take you to Nometheog. I told him that you were weak, but now that I can smell your blood, I understand. It's powerful, and I want it. These wolves can be a snack, but you are a meal, an addiction. I crave you!"

Galan let out an involuntary gasp of horror as he felt the needle pierce his neck. As the creature raised his other hand, needles of black poison protruding from his fingertips, there was a distraction. An arrow tore through the rotting flesh of the creature's arm and it turned to where it flew from. A group of people stood on the slopes above them. A volley of arrows raced down. One pierced the thing's gut and blood burst forth as his belly popped, blood gushed over the ground and splattered all over Galan, instantly soaking him. The sound that emanated from the creature then filled the forest with a piercing cry that wavered with the buzzing. There was a cry from the people as they raced forward and they each hacked at him until he lay in pieces, blood soaking into everything around him. Galan reached up to pull the needle from his neck. He pulled it out and threw it to the ground, but then he could only stand back and watch as he remembered his own fight with his father. His thoughts replaying that moment even as he watched different things pass before him.

He saw his father in the murderous rage filling their eyes, and he saw himself. He could only stare, and was barely aware of what was happening as Saltook pulled him away from the scene. It was a few minutes before he could regain a sense of where he was and what was happening, as he sat in front of a rock house by the river bank, his hands bound, blood smearing his vision as it dripped from his hair. He looked up at a blonde-haired man staring down at him.

"Who are you?" the man asked, a firm grip on his sword.

Galan was silent as he cursed himself for not remembering all the gods that his mother taught him about. He wanted to remember them now because he wondered which god would be the most useful to him. He had pulled the needle out, but he still felt the burning, bulging blackness in his neck as it started tracing through his veins.

XX. Reunion

Kim peered around as the elevator doors opened. They were in the main transit area. Different elevators, escalators, and stairs led up and down through a large floor of the citadel. The main doors were at the very end of the passage, but there were smaller ones lining the sides. Now that the power was working, it was noisy. The transit area was designed like a large, intimidating station for various means of transportation. There were railings along the walkway, so that they could peer down and see buses, trains, and cars on the levels below. If they looked up, there were helicopters on platforms just outside the windows, with stairs and ladders reaching up to them through large, tinted windows.

"Let's go back down through the stairs we came up," Kim said. "There's going to be creatures, no matter which way we go, but I think we have a good chance of making it back that way."

Michael nodded. They cautiously stepped forward, keeping an eye out for any movement around them. When they were finally through the door to the stairwell, Kim felt herself breathe again. Michael nodded, understanding the feeling. He patted her shoulder.

"Come on," he urged. She nodded and they moved forward. They made their way back down the steps, through the warehouse, the loading dock, and the streets outside. Finally, they reached the office building. A pale, red dawn was starting to shine high above them. There was an alarm squealing. It had been activated when the lights turned on. Kim took out her gun and shot it. There was a horrid sound as if it were squealing off key, then it stopped. They ran forward and followed the path that Shiana had laid out for them at the beginning. When they went through the door, they were delighted to see Teri waiting at the desk.

She stood up and gave each of them a hug.

"They didn't make it, did they?" s he asked them.

Kim shrugged. Michael looked from one to the other. "We're going back for them, right?" he asked.

Kim nodded slowly. "It would feel wrong to leave them," she said.

Teri motioned to the fairy, sleeping on top of Teri's coat. "We need to let her wake up. Thank her for the power. All I did was open a door. She did the rest, but I think it nearly drained her completely."

Michael nodded, "We'll wait," he said, "besides, Sassy is on her way with the troll."

They waited and after a few moments, their friends came into the room. Traegar had to hunch down and almost got stuck walking through the door frame. Sassy hugged them all, tears in her eyes.

"Aqualon closed the portal. He sent us when he said Shiana's thoughts were cut off." Sassy looked around at the others. "She's okay, right? And where's James?"

Michael crossed his arms and sighed heavily. "We got separated."

Kim nodded. "Yeah," she said. "Hero here thought he was saving them by cutting us off from them."

Sassy put her hands on her hips. "Well, that doesn't matter really. We just have to get them back. Do you have any idea where they are?" she asked.

Kim nodded. "I do, but if we go in there, the chances are slim. There're new things in there, and..." she scrunched up her face trying to make sense of the small bit of image that had come to her on the floor with the blood stains,

"...something else, someone else, that we haven't dealt with before. We might not make it out. Any of us."

"Well, Shiana has put her life on the line for me more than once. I'll repay the favor any way I can," said Sassy. "Now let's go!"

"Wait," said Kim. "We can't go in blindly. We need a plan."

"We have a plan," said Sassy. "We go where they are. We find them, and we destroy every mahldrusec in our path on the way. When we have them, we get the hell out of there, and go back to Aqualon."

"As much as that plan sounds good, it's not," said Kim. "Sassy, you'll need to look like a Mahldrusec. Pretend you're taking us there."

"Traegar can turn into metal. She can take one of us, too," said Sassy.

Traegar beat her chest in approval of the plan.

"Please though, let Iluma rest before we go. She will be useful," said Teri. She walked over to where the fairy lay on the coat.

"The longer we wait…" Michael started.

Teri looked at him, "Please," she interrupted. "We need her to at least be awake."

"I'll give her thirty minutes. That's all the time I'm willing to spare," said Kim.

"Thank you," said Teri.

XXI. Darkhan

Xandra and Shiana entered the floor where Darkhan was keeping James. Xandra pulled Shiana behind her, holding tight to her arm. As soon as they entered the hallway, Shiana felt a chill in the air. The lighting was red. A trail of blood led down the hall. Xandra followed the trail, passing mahldrusecs as she walked. Some were the new, beastly ones; others were the sleek, older versions. They passed doors, windows, and strange looking equipment.

Shiana did not want to know what the equipment was used for. Most of it was smeared or splattered with blood. Finally, Xandra came to the end of a hall and pushed open a great, metal door. Xandra slowed her steps, using caution as she walked. There were rows upon rows of tables. Some were empty, some held mahldrusecs, others held dead bodies or parts of bodies. A few were empty and blood stained.

Shiana covered her nose and forced down the sick feeling rising into her chest. The stench of blood and decay hung heavy in the air.

Xandra peered around the room. She did not see James. She turned and walked up a staircase that led to an observation deck looking over the room.

She led Shiana to a rounded desk where heavy, electronic equipment was placed on the table. Several large screens were placed in a semi-circle of the desk. Shiana felt a heavy drop in her stomach when she recognized James on one of the monitors.

"That's Darkhan," Xandra pointed to the other figure on the screen, which Shiana had not noticed before. He was hard to see, hooded, cloaked, and like a shadow that blended into the background.

"We need to save James," Shiana said. "Are we too late?"

Xandra shrugged, then grabbed Shiana again, dragging her behind as she walked. She stopped outside of a small, black door. It was closed. Xandra tried the handle, and the door swung open.

"I'm busy," Darkhan's voice sounded from across the room.

"I need that one," said Xandra.

There was a sigh, coupled with a growl. "Well, so do I," he said. Shiana was silenced as Xandra's hand covered her mouth, while simultaneously holding her in a dizzying headlock, so that it was impossible to speak.

"I have orders to take him. How much longer will you be?" she asked. There was a pause.

"I'll let you know," he said. Darkhan lifted his arm, slamming the door with magical force. Xandra released Shiana who was trying not to cry.

"I don't think he's killing him," Xandra said. "We will wait."

Shiana shook her head. "That's not good enough! I have to help him."

"We will wait," Xandra said again, more firm.

Shiana shook her head and reached for the doorknob. She was immediately knocked back with enough force that she slid across the floor.

"You don't realize what you are doing," Xandra said, quickly coming to stand over her. "Darkhan will not only bury you, he can do much worse. We stand a chance if you obey me."

Shiana shook her head, still lying on the floor, trying to gather herself after the forceful hit from Xandra. "I can't stand by while this happens," she said, gaining her feet.

Just then, the door opened. Xandra back-handed Shiana and the Selbdes was almost floored again, and then Xandra grabbed her arms pinning them behind her back. Shiana sensed that it was for a show.

The women could feel Darkhan's eyes staring into them with a heavy, foreboding feeling as he walked forward. He walked over to them, and stared at the scene before him.

"What are you doing with her? You've got one of the most wanted, and we are nowhere near done with them," he said, looking at Shiana, with his red eye glowing from underneath his hood. "Does Shekley know that she's been moved from her room?"

Xandra just looked at him. "My orders were to take her and bury her alive."

Darkhan pulled his hood back. His face was disfigured from deep scars running slanted from his forehead through his face and down through his neck. On the normal side of his face his eye was cold and blue, the other eye was artificial, red, and alight. He glared at them through long, black hair. Shiana felt uneasy under his gaze.

"And who gave you the orders?" he asked. "Nometheog? Shekley?"

"Shekley," replied Xandra.

He shook his head, and reached out to Shiana. Xandra jerked her away.

Darkhan placed his hands together patiently, and set his gaze on Xandra. "The Shadow has left Shekley at the moment. I'm sure he was commanding you the best that he could, but I see Nometheog's will," he said. "Nometheog wants this one and he says that I can have her."

Xandra pulled Shiana away as Darkhan reached out again. "My orders were clear," she said, defiantly.

"He's wanted her from the start. The only thing better would be David. Nometheog wouldn't change his plan now."

"I was told to take her along with the other one, and bury them alive. That is all I know. I'm doing what I was ordered to do."

"No, you're not!" he exclaimed. "Not if I stop you."

"You don't want to test me," Xandra warned.

"Oh, but I do," he said.

Xandra pointed her hand at him, and the next instant, it was a gun. The sound of the shot shook the room, but it did not hit Darkhan. Something across the room sizzled and sparked as the bullet hit. Darkhan seemed to dissolve into the shadows and then he was behind them. Shiana screamed with fear as he grabbed her from behind with a cold, firm grip. Xandra's elbow made contact with his face and he was thrown back, his grip on Shiana failing. Xandra was fast and strong with an uppercut to his gut. He vanished again, then reappeared across the deck. He whispered an incantation and the floor beneath Shiana's foot began growing into a black, metal, thorny vine. It wrapped itself around Shiana's leg. She pulled at it, but it writhed up her body, squeezing and burning as it twisted around her. Xandra reached out and pulled the device from Shiana's head, before attempting to cut the vine.

Shiana let out a scream of pain, but then instinctually found her friends. Michael was the first mind she reached. His relief at hearing her voice gave her hope as Xandra cut through the vine, releasing her from its' grasp. Darkhan had vanished again. His laughter echoed around them. Suddenly, the observation deck seemed to be on fire as cold, black flames licked up the walls and began spreading towards them. Shiana was relieved to hear her friends coming for her.

Xandra kept her eyes open wide for any sign of the necromancer and stepped away from the flames, pulling Shiana with her as she freed her from the remaining tendrils of the vine. She edged to the room where James lay on the table and they stepped through the door, catching a glimpse of Darkhan dissolving again into shadow, his laughter echoed through the room. The device was pulled away from the back of James' head and clanged loudly on the floor as Darkhan was hidden again. James slowly raised himself to a sitting position.

"Shiana?" he asked, weak from sleep and drugs.

"James!" she called as she ran forward to him.

"NO!" he exclaimed, with weak alarm. "Stay back! He's done something to me." She could hear the tears of fear and panic in his voice.

Shiana slowed. "James, whatever he's done, we will get you out of here. I'm not leaving without you. The others are coming." As she came closer, she could feel a deep, throbbing pain from where the vine had touched her. It burned into her.

Shiana tried to reach out to her friend, but as she came towards him, the wounds that she had taken from the vine and Xandra became deep wounds. She knelt down, clutching her leg in an attempt to stop the pain. James slid off the table and backed away with tears in his eyes. With each step away that he took, Shiana's pain lessened.

"He did it to me. I'm sorry, Shiana. Go. Leave me here. I can only hurt you." She shook her head.

"No, it's not you. There was a vine…," she said in denial.   As she tried to come closer again, the pain was unbearable as the wounds from the vine began tearing open as if the vine were still crawling up her.

She fell and rolled over onto her back, grabbing her leg where blood now seeped from the wound.   Xandra grabbed her and pulled her away.   As she got further from James, the wound healed back. She sat on the floor, shaking, looking at James with terror and sympathy.

"James," she said. "I'm going to help you. I'm going to find a way."

He shook his head. "Just go, before he gets you too." Xandra walked forward, holding the contraption that she had removed from Shiana.

"He's using your gift against you. Try this," she said, "then come with me."

Shiana nodded to James to do as Xandra said. Xandra slipped the device onto him and then grabbed him.

"You're both coming with me now," she said, reaching out to grab Shiana. The black, shadow flames roared higher outside the door, and as Xandra turned to leave, Darkhan stood in the doorway, blocking their exit. The flames seemed not to harm him. It was as if he was an extension of them.

"You're not going anywhere," he said.

Xandra extended her arm into a spear, and aimed it for him. She felt her weapon graze the side of his ribs as he dodged the full point. He let out a surprised grunt then vanished again, the flames edging further into the room. Xandra backed the others away from the flames, then turned to them.

"If I fail, it will be the first time," she said. "Stand back," she ordered them. "I must do as I was ordered."

She walked forward, into the dark flames, their cold fire embedding into her. Suddenly, Darkhan was behind her, the black dagger plunged into her back. She spun around, knocking him away from her as her elbow made contact with him. He was knocked to the floor with his dagger still in his hand. She leapt, aiming her bladed hand at him, landing hard on the spot where he lay, but missing again as he vanished, then reappeared a few steps away. A small piece of black cloth lay torn beneath the point of her spear.

"Where are your loyalties, really?" he asked as he reached down to her again, a whip of dark fire entangling her neck. "Nometheog is not pleased. In fact, he's grown tired of you."

She reached out with her hand as her gun fired at him again, but once more he vanished before the bullets could hit. The whip released when he disappeared.

He was across the room, at the control panels where the monitors showed the various rooms and places of interest to him. There was a look of shock that overcame him as he looked at the monitors, and a look of bitterness and hatred fell over his face. He pulled up his hood, turning to her. "I was wrong," he said. "I didn't see it coming, and I was wrong. There's another, one greater than Shiana that Nometheog desires." Xandra ran forward, but then he vanished into shadow, and the floor began to quickly grow into a wall of tangled black, metal vine, blocking her in. She turned back to go retrieve the others, cursing him with her every   thought.

XXII. The Old Acquaintance

The three women approached the tall, black gate that stood before them. It reached high into the sky above them. Celeste shivered, but it was not from cold. She dismounted her horse, and turned to the others.

"We need to send the horses back," she said. "I don't think that they will be of much use to us in there." She could feel the fear emanating from her own mare. She patted the creature on the nose.

"You have been an excellent steed, now go home and rest," she said. She removed the things that she needed and then sent the horse back home. Carmina and Arista did the same with their horses. The creatures ran away at a quickened pace, glad to be leaving the barren lands.

The three women stared up at the gate in front of them, feeling reluctance to enter. There were no words passed between them, but there was an all-encompassing fear that they felt coming from within the gates. The women readied their weapons, Celeste breathed deeply and nodded. They slowly and carefully stepped through the gates, looking around and taking in the scenery. The morning sun was shining on the road, turning the black to a silver. As they gazed out over the city, the tops of the black buildings were illuminated by sunlight, but then it was a great, dark chasm below.

"Which way?" Arista asked.

"I don't know yet," Celeste said as she studied the city around her. Arista and her were both were reaching out to Arik, trying to find a trace of him, Arista through thought, and Celeste through soul, but both of them were feeling a strain to find him. Carmina looked up into the air, as a kraelvin soared above the citadel, landing on the roof.

"Straight ahead," said Carmina. They nodded and moved forward with Carmina leading them. She was ready in case they encountered danger. They walked forward, wary of what lay ahead. It took them some time to reach the citadel. It towered over them now, black and ominous. Its' size alone was dominating to look at. Celeste could sense that creatures guarded the entrance. The others were ready in case there was a need for weapons. Carmina stepped forward, readying her sword to defend the queen. The creatures, who were both made from animal, metal, and decaying flesh, sneered at her.

"What business do you have in the citadel?" they asked in unison, their voices low and growling. Celeste motioned for Carmina to put away the sword. She lowered it, but kept a firm grip on the handle.

"I am queen Celeste of Sark. I demand entry. A friend of mine was taken here and I wish to get him back."

The creatures looked at each other, their black eyes lighting up red, then they turned to her.

"Our lord is busy, but he sends an envoy to speak with you." Celeste nodded, and they waited in a tense silence with only the sound of the wind as it carved through the hollowness of the chasm beneath them.

Suddenly, the doors slowly began to open. At first, Celeste did not see anyone.

The creatures suddenly smiled with wicked ambition and then they formed weapons from their arms, leaping at the women. Carmina was quick with her sword, catching the ribs of the tiger-creature on her sword. She became locked into a fight with the beast, her sword stuck.

Arista and Celeste dodged the second creature, which seemed part leopard, as they quickly maneuvered to ready their weapons again. Then suddenly, a black whip entangled Celeste's leg. It was enhanced with dark fire and wrapping tightly around her, embedding the cold fire deep into her leg. She felt herself trip, her head slamming against the metal of the road. She lost a grip on her sword as she was pulled towards the entrance to the citadel. When the whip was released, she saw that a circle of black fire surrounded her. Carmina was shouting for her queen as she exchanged blows with the monster, who was determined to block her way forward.

A figure stepped from the flames over Celeste, tall and hooded. He reached out and grabbed Celeste up from the floor, tying her arms with the whip.

She was not quick enough to stop him. The dark fire was stopping her movement as it froze in her veins. The flames grew higher and higher around them until she was walled in with the figure. Nothing could be heard from within the flames. The fight outside was silenced, and all the sunlight disappeared.

She struggled to pull herself free, as he wrapped his fingers into her hair, and held a black blade to her throat with his other hand. Then he spoke. At the sound of his voice, her heart suddenly beating cold with panic. The voice was familiar and terrifying.

"It's been too long, my queen" he said mockingly. Celeste let out an involuntary squeal of pain as he pulled her hair tighter. "You've healed well after the fire. No harm done, after all," he laughed slightly. "I told you it wasn't personal. Just a means to an end."

"You will not harm me again," she said, through gritted teeth. "I am stronger now than I was then."

"No harm intended," he said. "Not from me. But Nometheog sees things differently. You interfere with his plans, and the world cannot be void if you are in it."

Celeste laughed then. That is all that she could do. She made a quick and powerful movement with her head, feeling the handful of hair ripping from her scalp. Darkhan felt a sting as blood seeped from his broken nose, his dagger falling. He instinctively reached up to grab his face as he stepped back. She managed to maneuver herself then, the dark fire from the whip still embedded in her leg and encasing her arms, to quickly move over and land, grabbing his dagger from the floor, cutting through the whip, which vanished into the wall of fire as it fell, becoming part of the flames. She dodged as he lunged at her, and she managed to ignore the pain of the dark fire to land a kick against his ribs, where he had already been wounded. Blood was spilling from the wound. He grabbed his side, but then lunged at her

223

yet again, falling onto her and pinning her to the ground, his hands wrapped around her throat. She fumbled for a moment, still gripping his dagger, and with a tight hold, she attempted to pull it upwards. She could feel the dark fire coming from within his hands, tracing its way through her neck, into her shoulders and chest.

"You are nothing but a distraction," said Darkhan, "and I will see you vanquished. Your power will not dominate me. I have worked too hard to have my void corrupted." She felt him squeeze harder against the flesh of her neck, squeezing the breath from her. She pulled with every bit of strength that she could muster and then felt him stiffen, the dark fire lessening as she finally managed to slide the blade into his skin, stabbing into his heart. Blood gushed from the wound, covering her hands, and he momentarily reached out to her face, but then he vanished with the flames.

The coldness of the dark fire remained, freezing her to her very bones with a deep, sharp pain.

Carmina rushed to her side as soon as she could enter where the flames had been.

"My queen!" she exclaimed, running to Celeste. The angel looked over at the fallen mahldrusecs lying by the doors outside, as she struggled to refill her breath. Tears were filling Celeste's eyes. Arista limped over to them as well, and the two began trying to help the angel gain her feet.

"Celeste?" Arista asked, knowing that something was wrong.

"My queen?" Carmina asked. "My queen!" She exclaimed, noticing the terrified look on Celeste's face. Celeste was silent for a long time, trying to purge the dark fire from within.

"It's Darkhan," she finally said. Her voice was weak. The strain of purging the dark fire was telling in her voice. "He's the one that's doing all of this. It's been him from the very beginning. He's caused all of this. He turned the hunters against us. He led the raid on the castle. He forged the letters that carried Victor away. He burned me at the stake. He used my blood in the spell required to send him through space and time. He's caused all of this, and I will see him ended." Carmina reached out to help the angel to her feet, and placed the queen's sword back in its' sheath.

"We can still turn back. You are wounded."

"I will heal," said Celeste, determined. "Right now, finding Arik is our priority. Do not concern yourself with me." They stepped toward the entrance then, Celeste and Arista both slowed as they limped forward, looking at their surroundings.

The main entrance was empty of mahldrusecs. It was a large, rectangular room with a tall ceiling, which had been caved in. Many doors were laid out in front of them on the sides of the rooms and across the way, some of them blocked by the caved in ceiling. There were stairways to the right and left, they curved so that whatever was at the top was obscured. Everything was black metal around them. There were various machines whirring loudly both along the walls and through the center of the room. Celeste was not sure what they were used for.

Monitors ran images across screens mounted to the walls. There were the words flashing across the bottom: MOST WANTED. She recognized some of the selbdes that she had seen in Kialo's holding cells. She felt herself happy that they were somewhere safer than here. Benches had been laid out between the doors, and there were tables close to the machines. She walked forward cautiously, glancing at the tables. They didn't seem unordinary in any way, but something about the placement to the machines was intimidating.

"Which way do you think we go now?" Carmina asked.

Celeste and Arista tried desperately to find Arik. Then they looked at each other with concern. "He's here but he has somehow changed," Celeste observed.

"I'm not giving up," Arista said. Then, she looked to Carmina. "He's up. He's high above us. He knows I'm looking for him, but he's trying to ignore me."

"There's some new purpose driving him forward. Something that he's trying to do," said Celeste. "He's hard to read. It's as if he's fighting us internally, hiding some secret, but I think I know how to find him."

"He doesn't want to be found," said Arista. "But he's alone, and afraid."

Celeste's tears ran red as she sensed then the changes taking place in him. "It's unimaginable!" she exclaimed. "He's pushing us away, but I think he needs us now, more than ever."

Darkhan stumbled from Shadow into his chamber, reaching for the first seat he could find. The blade had cut into him, but he would not die. Shekley could possibly help him, but first, he would attempt to heal himself.

He sat at his desk, panting from the exertion of movement as his breathing became shallow, pain winding into his heart. He looked at the various objects on the desk. He hated everything about Celeste at the moment, as memories flooded him. Old memories from long ago that he thought he had purged. He remembered the woman who had rocked him to sleep at night, the sound of her voice as she sang him nursery songs, the feeling she gave him when she hugged him, lifting him to the air, and spinning him around. He picked up the pendant where her soul rested, and anger like he had not been able to feel for many years spread through him. He wanted to crush the pendant into thousands of pieces, but that would be counter-productive. He patiently placed it back, his hands convulsing from the weakness spreading through him.

He prayed then, to Nometheog, as he fumbled for the black crystal in his robes. As his skin made contact, he felt the dark energy coursing through him, Nometheog's healing.

"Nometheog, great and powerful god, there is still much work to be done before I come to you," he said. "Please, allow me to progress your will. I do not wish to dishonor your great power. I have met a worthy opponent, and I beg for the means to destroy her." Dark healing traced itself from the crystal and began to fill him then. His heart began to beat steady, and his nose began to set itself. The blood from his ribs stopped flowing.

He knew that full healing would take time. When he found the strength to stand, he walked slowly to his bed. Then he laid there, letting the darkness fill his wounds, healing him, helping him forget that woman and his love for her, his anger, his pain.

He had almost faltered, the thoughts worried him as he lay healing, lingering between sleep and wakefulness. That woman was a weakness to him. Any thoughts of a mother, whether real or fostered, was a weakness. He wished to punish himself until that feeling of comfort and softness that she spread was gone from him completely. It invaded his own void, and he would see it ended for good.

It was a temptation, and nothing more. The idea that someone could care for him, whether as a mother or anything else, was not one that he had the luxury to entertain. The angel would have to die for making him remember such things.

He had attempted to kill her before, but this time he would be more powerful, and his plan would be more carefully laid out. He had still been learning his skills all those years ago. This time, he would see her obliviated; destroyed into complete darkness. He would have to meditate and clear himself of all those old memories, and cast them from his very soul, until he was one with the void again.

XXIII. New Purpose

Arik awoke feeling cold. It was an exciting, invigorating cold. The room he was in was all darkness, yet he could see clearly. He looked down at himself, shocked at the silver and black metal now tracing its way throughout him, some spots in patches. It didn't feel that much different from his own skin. Where his stomach had been sunken from starvation before, he now had back his familiar thin, but muscular, torso. Though, it was patched with silver and black metal. His skin was still dark gray, and white hair hung over his shoulders and down his back. He reached out to feel it with his metallic hands.

He knew that he should be afraid, and it worried him more that he was not afraid. He felt healthy and revitalized. He could see that he was changed. His hands and feet were no longer broken, and his hair felt silkier and smoother than the dry, brittle texture he had felt before.

"Arik," the goddess spoke, startling him. "You're awake at last," she growled.

He looked around the room, trying to see where she was, and then she was there, in front of him. He could only stare for a moment. Her appearance was terrifying, but arousing and beautiful at the same time. He had no way to describe her. She was beastly, horns protruded from her head. She stared at him with unblinking yellow eyes, and her body was red and covered in fur. Her only clothing was a black, chain dress that was held together by various piercings throughout her body. When she spoke, her lips curved back to show small, black fangs for teeth. She reached out to him with long, black, curved claws.

"How do you feel?" she asked him, tilting his chin up to her with the tip of her long, curved claw.

He just looked at her, unaware that his voice was repaired.

"Try it," she said, referring to his voice as her claws ran over his neck and throat. "Speak to me. How do you feel?"

"I..." Arik looked at the goddess in shock, and surprise. He had almost forgotten how to speak.

"Be truthful with me. Let me hear you speak. I desire to hear your voice," she said.

"I...feel...new," he said, trying to search for a word to describe it. His voice still sounded like what he thought his old voice sounded like but somehow changed.

The goddess grinned a big, black fanged grin of terrifying delight.

"You are a masterpiece," she said.

He looked at her, confused.

He was remembering the pain and the fear that he had felt earlier. The memory of it was fresh in his mind, but now it seemed worth it, to feel so good after suffering for so long.

"I told you. I can give it, but I can take it away, too."

"Forgive me," he said, still terrified to speak in her presence, "but what has happened to me?" he asked. "What am I exactly? And why of all the elves in the world, did you choose me?"

She smiled. "Wouldn't you like to know?" she asked. "Wouldn't you like to know all of my secrets?" Her claws traced where the metal had been laced through him. "I would tell you, but then I wouldn't have any fun left. My secrets are all I have that are still mine."

"To what purpose do you wish to use me?" he asked, trying to ignore the sensation of pleasure now tracing through him at the touch of Vishka's claws.

"I want you to leave this place. Go back to Shea, and when you are in Shea, I want you to remember what the sky goddess took from you. I want you to remember what I have given you. That is all."

Arik nodded, with understanding. "So, you would have me kill her, then?" he asked, getting to the point.

Her smile widened. "Only if that is your desire," she said. "Sometimes, death is too merciful of a sentence. Do to her whatever you wish, but make it worth my time. I have risked a lot in helping you."

"What if I do kill her?" Arik asked.

"You've studied more lore than any other elf. I think you know what will happen." Her claws traced through his hair.

Arik nodded. He understood now. There was a reason the gods in their history had changed so much.

Soon after their discussion, the goddess left him. He needed to find the way out of the city and figure out a way into Shea, since he could not make portals any more. Part of him wished that the goddess would have stayed longer. He felt alone and overwhelmed, but his motivation was driving him now.

He searched the room and found an outfit like the other mahldrusecs wore. It was the black military clothes of Trost. He clothed himself and then he searched for an entrance. He stopped halfway across the room. He could feel his sister. She was here, seeking him out. Trying to delve into his thoughts. He didn't have his telepathy, but he didn't want her intruding in his mind. She would be better off never knowing what he had been through. He also didn't want her knowing what he was up to. She would only try to stop him. He tried to empty his mind of any thought at all as he continued his search.

There was a large set of double doors on the opposite side of the room. They were black and blended into the wall. He walked up and pushed them open. The halls were lit with florescent lighting. He squinted as the light blinded him. It took his body only seconds to adjust, and suddenly the light was lessened as black filters fell over his vision. He moved forward, trying to figure out where he was. The doors slammed behind him. The hallway turned ahead of him. All he knew to do was to follow it, so he moved forward.

He knew he was in the city, but he had no map or resource to help him, other than his own instinct. He already knew that his ability to make portals was still gone as well as his telepathy, but he was thankful to have his voice and someone on his side, even if it was such an unexpected ally as Vishka.

Kristiniva would die, but he would see that the pain she felt was exponentially more severe than his own suffering. That would please Vishka, but it would please him even more. As he walked forward, he walked with a new and powerful purpose, and he could think of nothing that he wanted more.

He came to an elevator. It opened as he walked by it as if guiding him out.

"Celeste is here. We're going to help you!" his sister's voice intruded again. "You just have to let us in, Arik! Let us in!"

He tried to think of nothing again. Thoughts of Celeste and his sister coming here for him made him worry, but he couldn't let them find him. He studied the buttons on the panel and soon figured out how it worked. He was one step closer to getting out.

XXIV. The Rescue Attempt

Xandra turned and walked back to the others. They sat on the table. James was leaning on Shiana for support, and Shiana was resting her leg. James was no longer a threat to Shiana with his abilities blocked. They looked at Xandra expectantly as she walked back into the room, appearing out of the flames, but she didn't say anything. She let her hands reform to their real physical shape, the spear and gun now gone.

The flames still roared outside the door and along the wall that faced the door, but they had not slipped any further into the room, their advance had been stopped when Darkhan had vanished to whatever business had awaited him.

"Where is he?" James asked.

Xandra turned her gaze to them. "I never know. He comes and goes. The Shadow gives him his power. He has been summoned elsewhere for now."

"The others are on their way," Shiana said, putting an arm around James who appeared to be in quickly declining health, his skin looking pale, and his eyes glazed over from being drugged. He nodded his head.

"They'll have to get through Darkhan's flames," said Xandra. "That is something that I am not equipped to destroy. Unless they can get through them, we are stuck here. I can enter them. They do not hurt me, but they will destroy you both."

"So, how do we get out of here?" Shiana asked.

Xandra turned to face the door. "We wait for him to come back," she said, "and then I will be ready for him."

That's when Shiana noticed the wound where Darkhan had stabbed the mahldrusec. Blood seeped from within the metal.

"Xandra," she said, "you're hurt!"

Xandra shook her head. "It doesn't hurt. I'm not in pain. Besides, assuming that I make it back to him, Shekley will fix me." She crossed her arms then, thinking and planning against Darkhan for when he returned. James lay down on the table.

"I'm just resting," he said to Shiana. She could tell that he would not make it out on his own. Whatever Darkhan had done to him had almost killed him, and for all she knew, it was still working into him.

"Wake me up when you need to," he said, "but don't leave me again," he said. A tear fell from Shiana's eye and she nodded her reply but turned away to wipe the tear. She wrapped her hand in his.

"Sleep," she said, "I'll be right here." They waited. It was a long wait. Xandra just stared at the door, keeping her arms folded. Every once in a while, she would glance around, as if searching for Darkhan, but then she would stare back at the door. James was asleep, and Shiana kept reaching out to David.

He was on their beach at night. He was an emotional mess. The message from his brother seemed to have broken his heart. His thoughts were rushed. They were sad and angry, but there was hope.

"I knew he wasn't lost. We can still save him."

Shiana agreed, but finding out how to do that would be difficult. "We are no closer to finding out the Shadow's specific plans," she said. "We know that they are creating these new mahldrusecs, but we don't know anything solid. We came all this way, and we still…"

"Don't finish that thought," said David. "My brother can be saved. That's the best news I could have gotten. That gives me reason enough to keep trying, whatever it takes. We know more than we did when you went in. Hopefully, the information that you gave me will be enough for the gods."

"One can only hope," Shiana said.

The selbdes began their journey at a regular pace, with Kim and Sassy in the lead. Michael and Teri were close behind them, with Iluma still resting in Teri's pocket. Traegar stepped behind the group. They made it to the citadel with minimal problems. There were times when hiding was necessary, even with taking the course that Teri and Iluma had taken before. They had all agreed that it was the best way when Teri informed them that there was a maintenance elevator near the door. They stepped inside in groups. Kim, Sassy, and Michael were the first group into the elevator. They took it up to the floor where Kim thought that James and Shiana were. Sassy immediately covered her nose when they stepped off the elevator.

"This place reeks," she whispered, then she immediately changed herself into a mahldrusec, to avoid being noticed.

"It sure does. As soon as I get somewhere safe, I'm showering," Kim whispered back. They walked forward with Sassy taking the lead. She grabbed the others by their wrists, forcefully, as if she were escorting them to their deaths.

"Which way?" she asked Kim telepathically, peeking down the wings that splintered off from the main corridor.

"Keep it straight," Kim whispered. They passed numerous mahldrusecs as they went forward, then suddenly they could hear Shiana. Sassy stopped for a moment, then nodded. Her friend was alive, but in danger. She had to get to her. They heard the others coming up behind them. When Sassy briefly peeked behind her, she saw that Traegar appeared to be made of black metal. She was carrying Teri slung over her shoulder. She assumed that Iluma was still resting in Teri's pocket. She pushed the massive, black doors open, and Sassy loosened her grip on Kim and Michael. She immediately was overwhelmed at the sight of the bodies and blood laid out on the tables. She could only look at them in horror. Michael pulled her to him, shielding her face, as she shook to hold back tears. Her mahldrusec form was faltering.

"Get it together," said Kim. "We're almost there. Up the steps to that observation deck, take a left, then there's a black door further down on the right, but there's something blocking us from going that way." The others looked up. Traegar stomped up the stairs and stalled near the top, then turned to them, shaking her head.

"Dark Fire," her voice roared beast-like and deep, vibrating through the room. "Get Iluma," she said. Teri opened up her coat pocket, and pulled out the fairy, who was awake, but laying in exhaustion, as she interpreted Traegar's words for her friends.

"What can she do?" Michael asked.

"We need light," said Traegar.

Iluma fluttered up the stairs to Traegar, speaking in her native language.

Teri interpreted. "She's weak, but she will attempt to help us. Dark fire is made from Shadow, and to put it out, one needs true light. Thankfully, for us, she has some."

Iluma looked at the dark fire hoping that she had the power left in her to extinguish the flames. She managed to shine then, her glow becoming brighter, and then she began to grow in size until she was taller than the others. Her wings seemed to be made of pure, white light. She spread them, fluttering with effort, and instead of wind with each movement, light cast forth, and the dark fire was pushed away.

She began screaming orders to Teri. "Go, I can't get them all, but I can give you a path. Call for your friends to run towards us."

Teri quickly shouted her words to the others as she made her way into the path between the flames. They were close behind her, calling out to Shiana. Suddenly, their path was blocked again. A wall of black, metal vine was growing up from the floor. Traegar immediately grabbed it.

It seemed as if the wall absorbed her, but then there was an opening, large enough for someone to fit through. They all stood back as Iluma flew forward, driving back the flames on the other side of the wall.

When there was a clear path out of the room, Shiana and James ran through the door, followed by Xandra. Kim aimed her weapons at Xandra, but told the others to let her pass. She walked by, with not a word or a look at any of them. She stopped when she reached the bottom of the stairs. Michael was quick to grab James and give him a shoulder to lean on when he saw him stumbling. Sassy, still in her mahldrusec form, lifted Shiana and threw her over her back. The selbdes ran back down the stairs, with Traegar

quickly forming back to herself, as the hole in the vine closed

up behind her. She just did make it to the stairs, away from

the flames, when Iluma suddenly lost her light and fell to the

stairs, tiny and withered, a dark grey color. Teri grabbed her

and pocketed her again. Suddenly, alarms blared around

them, and they heard the creatures outside coming towards

the door, great, earsplitting roars tearing through the air.

Xandra turned to them.

"There's a back exit," she said. She pointed towards

a dark hall that was almost hidden under the stairs. "Keep

following that. You'll find an elevator at the end of the hall.

Take it to the ground floor. You will come out at a main

parking deck. I recommend stealing a vehicle."

"Why are you helping us?" asked Kim.

"I'm not," she said. "I'm coming with you. I'm just

giving you a head start on the wounded. I was told to take

Shiana out of the city. I have never failed to secure an order," she said. "When this door opens, I will not be able to stop them. I cannot let them know my task." Sassy put Shiana down next to the wall, and formed herself fully into one of the older, sleek mahldrusecs. Kim drew her guns. Michael motioned for Shiana to help him with James. He was so weak that he couldn't hardly stand, even with help. He leaned his head against the wall, next to Shiana.

"We can do this," Michael said. "You two, see if you can make it to the elevator and secure us a ride, like she said." Shiana nodded. Michael looked at James.

"You're going to make it out," he said, determined to make it happen.

"Teri, go with them," Kim said. "That fairy needs to rest, too," she said as she loaded her gun.

Teri nodded, pulled out the weapon that she had found in the maintenance room, and held her arm out to help Shiana hold up James.

"Come on," she said, just before the giant, black doors burst open. There was roaring, growling, guns, and an array of ear-splitting sounds that erupted into the room. Michael fired shots, but then there was an explosion nearby. Teri did not stop to see if anyone else was wounded. She tried to hold up James' weight as she braced herself against the wall, covering her head as shrapnel flew past her. Metal parts were bending and scraping against the metal of the wall, sending sparks screeching by. Shiana had no choice but to let go of James and duck to the floor as a piece of the stairs above them dislodged and stuck into the wall where her head had just been. Teri propped James on her shoulder, and moved as quickly as she could through the hall, carrying the extra weight with difficulty.

Shiana was keeping up, though limping beside of her, as Teri held James up on her shoulder, dragging his weight with her. Shiana had pulled her guns, and fired a few shots before speeding ahead, still limping, to hit the button on the elevator. She stepped in, quickly hitting the button for the ground floor and holding the door, but then her hand was pulled back, and the doors closed. Shiana saw only the terrified look on Teri's face before she was forcefully turned around to stare at a mahldrusec.

Arik pushed her violently against the wall, holding tightly to her wrist that held the gun with his left arm, his right arm to her neck. She squirmed beneath his grip. He looked her over, recognizing her from the king's celebration in Shea. His heart leaped at his good luck.

"You're one of the selbdes!" he exclaimed. "I'm not like the other things in here. I belong in Shea, and I need you to take me with you if you are returning to Shea," he said, looking down at her.

Shiana just stared at him. He could feel her in his head, searching for some reasoning in his mind.

"Don't make me beg," he said, pressing his arm into her neck. "You are going there, aren't you?"

She didn't say anything.

"Please, help me!" he pleaded.

She looked perplexed, and a look of realization passed over her.

"*The goddess*," she said. "*She's done all this*," she said. He heard the words in his mind. Arik nodded.

"Take me with you, and I will help you," he said.

"*Okay!*" she agreed, speaking in his mind because her breathing was being cut off at her throat. "*I'll let you come with us.*" Only then did he release his hold on her as she gasped for breath, clutching her bruised throat and collapsing to the floor.

The doors opened on the ground floor. Arik hit the buttons again that led up with a fist.

"You better keep your word," he said, still towering over her. She nodded and he slowly stepped back, leaning on the opposite wall from her and folding his arms. He observed her for a moment, as she rubbed at her throat, still catching her breath.

"I'm sorry if I hurt you," he said, with regret strong in his tone. "I just...I don't know my own strength right now."

"It's okay," she said as she wheezed. "I can feel your thoughts. I know your intent. You can trust me," she said, a hoarseness had formed in her voice.

He just stared at her, his eyes appearing black from the filters. Without his telepathy, it was difficult for him to discern anyone's intent.

"I trust no one," he said. "Not after what I've been through."

She just nodded her understanding, and then the doors opened up. Teri was using the gun that she had retrieved from the maintenance room. It fired electricity, which zig-zagged through the corridor, shocking anyone in its' path. Shiana held the door as Arik stepped out and reached down to pull James, who was lying on the floor, into the elevator. He was now completely unconscious. They looked out into the hall. Three of the animalistic creatures still had visible electricity firing through them as they shook in place.

"Come on!" Shiana yelled at Teri. She turned to join them, and then slipped into the elevator. Arik was already headed down the hallway. He reached out at the first creature that he came to, feeling his new gifts awakening. A new feeling emerged from within the tops of his forearms, and suddenly, large, four-foot spikes emerged from the tops of his wrists, sliding over the tops his hands. He impaled the creature as black, blood-like ooze slithered from the wounds. He kicked with his feet, sliding the blades out as they retracted into his arms. The wiring within the creature sizzled. The thing slashed at him with its own device, a double-edged blade that protruded from its' own arms. Arik parried with one arm, a thin, razor-like blade that ran the length of his forearm, along the side, had suddenly drawn itself in protection. He aimed for its' head with his other hand. The spike reappeared. He buried it into the creature's forehead, right between its' eyes. Then he was surprised to feel a surge of power creep into him. He wasn't sure what it was or how he would use it. The creature collapsed to the floor. Michael appeared out of the darkness of the hall and Arik dodged the bullet that came his way.

"No," he heard Shiana shout. "No, he's helping us. Come on!" Michael nodded to Arik and then ran towards the elevator, with Sassy close behind him, followed by Traegar. Arik ran forward, into the fight. With each movement that he made, there seemed to be a new weapon emerging from within him. Some of them were blades, others were guns. He found that he was equipped with both fire and ice. His feet allowed him fast movement. He was at each creature before they could prepare a strike against him.

Some were frozen, others burning with bright and sudden fire. He lashed out at each creature he came to until there were none left. With each one, he felt a surge of power within him. He felt himself rising up with large, black wings expanded from his back. He looked below at the wreckage that lay spread over the floor, feeling a mix of emotions.

Kim and Xandra, seeing that all the creatures were felled, left running towards the elevators. Arik followed them, descending slowly, his weapons receding back into place. The three of them slipped into the crowded elevator, where Teri held the door for them. Their panting and exhausted sighs were the only sounds until the doors opened again.

They stepped out into the parking deck. Michael and Sassy lifted James, carrying him between them in their arms. Shiana looked at Xandra for guidance. Xandra motioned towards one of the large trucks.

"It's armored," she said. "We stand a better chance of escape if we use that."

Kim stepped up. "I can drive it," she said, pulling open the front door and getting inside. "But there's no key, Teri," she yelled.

"I've got it," the selbdes responded. They each climbed in, Kim at the steering and Teri beside her, placing her hand on the dash. In moments, the engine was firing up, and the computerized screen was being overtaken by conversation with Teri. The back door slammed down into a ramp. There were ten seats along the walls.

Sassy turned back into her regular form as she walked in, helping Michael carry James as they strapped him into the seat between them. Shiana and Arik followed. Traegar filled three seats by herself, hunching down to try and make herself smaller. Xandra stepped in last. The ramp closed and soon they were pulling out of the parking deck, traveling down the side road that paralleled the citadel.

Shiana placed a hand on Arik's shoulder, causing him to flinch.

"Thank you," she said. He just nodded, stuck in his own thoughts.

XXV. Victor's Return

Slatkin's dreaming had ended. He was here now, or as here as he could be at the moment. He knew she wouldn't see him. He could see her clearly, though. He watched her sleeping, but it was only through his angelic eyes. His mortal eyes, that humanity that he had learned to love, had been cast away with his body. He sensed her dreams turning dark without him. She was sad, and worried.

"There's nothing that you can do for her right now." His father's voice sounded from the door. "This quest will be difficult. I've tried it before, but your siblings all failed. She will be here when you return, and the quicker you return, the quicker you shall see her."

Slatkin looked at her again, trying to make sense of the many swirling colors of light that he saw dancing through her soul. He resisted the urge to touch her hair. He knew it wouldn't feel the same in this form.

"It's time," Saigolai sounded sad. Slatkin traced a finger along Belle's arm. She stirred in her sleep, and his father pulled him out of the room before she could wake.

"You have had your dream time," his father said. "Now it is time to work." His father's voice sounded stern, as if by touching her he was breaking some unknown rule, and he was being scolded.

Slatkin nodded his obedience. "I understand what I have to do, but why do you entrust this to me? There are still others who have not tried."

His father smiled knowingly. "That's true, son, but not many. I am choosing you because you are the only one with a light to find your way back."

Slatkin understood then, more than he ever had before. He nodded his understanding and smiled then, looking deep into his father's eyes, as the god gave his son a shove, and then all went black, and quiet, and numb as Saigolai cast Slatkin into the void.

Belle had awoken from a dream that she did not want to awaken from. She had dreamed of Slatkin every night, and she missed him in the depths of her soul. Something had gone wrong, though. She couldn't explain it, but there was something that was not right. She awoke to a dark room, but she felt something there, as if someone had brushed a finger down her arm. She sat up, and lit a candle, but there was no one there.

"Evingh?" she called. He didn't answer her. She got out of bed and dressed quickly, then headed towards the kitchen. As she walked through the hallway, the light swayed on the wall as if her candle flickered, but when she looked down at the candle it burned steady and bright. The sensation did not scare her. It was not a darkness that flickered. It was a light, a sign. She felt in her heart that in some way, it was her love, her Slatkin.

"Please be alright," she said. She didn't care if it seemed silly, her speaking to someone that wasn't there. She had felt him there, but the feeling left her as soon as it had arrived, and the hallway was suddenly cold and dreary-feeling again.

She continued her way to the kitchen, prepared to light a fire, but was pleased that it was already lit, and the water was already set over it. There was an aroma of something good in the air. She had been teaching Evingh her cooking skills and smiled when she saw him already at the table, grinding ingredients. She had not expected him to sleep much, not after what Slatkin had done to him.

"Did you sleep well?" she asked. She knew that he didn't, but she always asked, hoping that one night he would tell her yes.

He shook his head.

"What are you attempting this morning?" she asked.

"Kial root, but seasoned with heith." he said. Belle smiled.

"Did you sleep at all?" she asked.

He shook his head. "I spent my day looking for the heith."

She nodded then. "Thank you for starting the fire, and collecting the water," she said.

He only nodded.

"Do you need some help?" When he didn't respond, she continued. "I've been a cook in this castle for many, many years. I have not had a single night or day that I have not cooked something.

"There's a first time for everything," he said.

She nodded. "Very well," she said. "I'll be reading since I have the evening off." She walked over to her chair by the hearth and pulled out her cookbook, browsing the pages, but with some reserve. To fully immerse herself in its' magic, she would have to be alone.

Victor moved Dexon forward at a quick but steady pace. The pale light of Dawn had begun to shine on the land, turning the snow into a pale, glittering pink. He did not stop until he had reached the castle. He walked Vortex to the stable to unsaddle him and make sure he was fed and taken care of.

Angelik stayed with him, helping him with the chores. She patted the black horse on the nose.

"He likes you," said Victor.

"And I like him," she said. "He's very loyal to you, did you know that?" Victor nodded.

"We've been through a lot. He may not look like it, but he's an old horse."

"Father, do you think Slatkin will be back?" she asked. "He usually takes care of the horses, doesn't he?"

Victor nodded. "He does," he said.

"Well, when is he coming back?"

Victor shook his head. "I don't know," he said. "I hope it is soon," he said. "I could use his guidance now."

Angelik grabbed the brush and brushed it through Dexon's fur, giggling. "He likes this," she said. Victor nodded.

"Only when you do it," he said with a smile as he gathered the blankets to keep Dexon warm.

When they left the stable, they headed to the castle. The door opened quietly, and he was surprised to see the young man sitting at the table, looking at him in shock from across the room.

"Evingh?" he asked. The ex-hunter nodded his head and then Belle was wrapping her arms around both of the angels.

"Victor! I'm so glad you're back! And my sweet child!" she exclaimed. "Come inside and get warm!" she said, helping the child out of the white fur coat that she wore.

Victor placed his own coat on the rack and then looked at her seriously.

"I hope you're ready to cook for a crowd," he said. "I suspect that we'll have guests soon."

"Did you find the children?" she asked, referring to the scithronians.

Victor nodded. "We did, but they're not coming yet. It's the hunters."

Belle gave him a shocked look. "Hunters?" she asked.

"Don't worry," he said. "I won't let them hurt you. They'll be answering to me and they're going to learn a new way of life," he said. "They're going to rebuild Sark for us." He turned then to Evingh, who seemed terrified. "You," said Victor. "I'm giving you a job. Forget whatever past you're changing from and help us," he said. "Until my personal attendant gets back, you will take his place."

Evingh looked terrified to answer. "What do I need to do for that?" he asked.

"It's simple," said Victor. "I give you orders, and you follow them."

Evingh nodded. "Okay," he said.

"You will refer to me as your king," said Victor.

"Yes, my king," he said.

Victor nodded. "Better," he said, then he stood and left the room. He would have to make sure that the hunters had places to sleep, food to eat, and something other than fighting to keep them entertained until the rebuilding started. He would see to it himself. The work would take his mind away from the worry that he was feeling. He couldn't think about what the world would be like if the others did not come back.

Belle smiled down at Angelik. "Tell me, princess, are you hungry?" she asked.

Angelik shook her head. "Not right now," she said, "but the others that are coming are. You might need to cook more. I'm going to go help my father," she said, and then she left to follow Victor. Belle put her hands on her hips and looked at Evingh.

"It looks like tonight will not be such a change after all." He sat down to grind more of the heith, and Belle crossed the room to join him.

XXVI. The Shadow in Shea

Amicus visited the stone that the Quirials guarded. Starla bowed when she saw him approach.

"May I pass to see my mother?" he asked.

Starla just looked at him solemnly. "I am under orders from my queen to turn away all who would visit."

Amicus did not have to show her his face for her to hear and understand the command that came through his robes. "Let me in, or you will pay with your life!"

She humbly motioned for him to touch the stone. As his hand came into contact with the black stone, there was a sensation of ice so cold that it burned, but there wasn't time to contemplate it. He found himself in a dark and frozen corridor. Not even the moon shone, yet he sensed wisps of cloud. After a moment, he felt Starla's touch.

"Here," she said, "This is what we have been using. Moonstones." He felt them press into his hand and at the thought of light, the room was illuminated. The quirials were sauntering about in furs and bundled in layers of clothes. The last time he had visited his mother, the elves were wearing light clothes that billowed out in the breezes that filtered through the halls. Now, the breeze had a severe bite to it. He could already feel the heaviness of the frost covering him in a fine layer as it misted around him. Black icicles hung from the ceilings and windows, and the walls were covered in layers of ice. Starla and Skyla both reached out to the god.

"Let us guide you," they said, and he felt himself floating forward, until he reached the door of his mother's chambers. A thick layer of black ice shone slick, and shiny against the moon stones that illuminated the corridor.

"Mother!" he called. "Answer my summons!" he demanded. "I wish to visit with you!"

He looked down at the Quirials. "How long has it been like this?"

"It started slowly," said Skyla.

"Shortly after she lost her angel," said Starla.

"And has she had any visitors?" he asked, his suspicions all but confirmed.

Starla shrugged. "She hasn't come out, only to demand things of us now and then, but mostly she's just locked herself in there and asked not to be disturbed."

"Leave now," said Amicus. "All of you. Leave. Not just the castle, but the realm. Take yourselves away to Sark and prepare for war. You will be called shortly."

"But…" Skyla started to protest.

"This place has been corrupted. Innocence has fallen, and you are not safe here any longer. Do not take orders from my mother."

"But..." Skyla started to protest.

"Leave!" he demanded. "Can't you understand? She is cohorts with Nometheog."

They stared at him in fear.

"Leave now if you value your souls."

The elves glided quickly away to warn the others. Amicus stepped back and then he commanded the very ice, "Break!" And then it fell into a cascade of black mirrors shattered on the floor. He banged on the door.

"Mother, it is I, your son! Let me in!"

Slowly, the door opened, but Kristiniva was somewhere across the room. The black ice had filled the room in a sleek, black shine, yet it was still hard to make out anything, even with the moon stones glowing.

"Mother?" he asked quietly.

"Son," she said, there was a small laugh, something reminiscent of a laugh anyway. "Yes, I had a son," she said.

"You HAVE a son. I'm here, mother, come to me." He could feel the goddess, moving about in the shadows, but she was too dark to see.

"My son," she said, "What brings you to visit me?"

"I was concerned for you," he said.

"My pain has subsided," she said. "For so long, it's all that I could feel. Now there is nothing. Just numbness."

"Tell me from the beginning. Tell me how you let this abomination in."

The laugh came again. "At first it was small. He asked me for favors, and I obliged because he came to me in the night, and his kisses filled me with a power that I had never felt before. I felt awakened and new. The darkness was not a lonely place, it was an exciting place, and his kisses welled deeper with each visit. I was always left wanting, waiting for our next encounter, and I did what he asked because I wanted more."

"When Sark flooded, he asked me to save the angel, so I did. Her power distracted me while she was here…hers was something not even he could fathom…I was safe when she was here. He couldn't touch me; he couldn't even tempt me…but then Justice took her back and I was left wanting again. The pain was so deep that I wanted oblivion, death. So, he came back with apologies, and each and every night I invited him deeper into me. My pain turned to numbness and then I spread my skies out and invited him, so he came to stay and he's been here with me ever since. He has been filling me. With each kiss, each embrace, I feel a dark wholeness that fills that space where she was, where her power clutched my heart."

"He's here now, then?" The messenger god asked.

He sensed her smile. "Yes," the laugh echoed again. It was not her own. Perhaps it was forced out of her by the darkness. "He's here. Can't you feel him?"

Amicus only nodded. "I'm going to help you, Mother. You need help."

"Maybe you just need a taste of what he can offer you."

Amicus held up his staff to block whatever the darkness had just thrown at him. There was a spark of light as it collided and then dissipated.

"No, mother. I'm saving you." He reached out and clutched her hand. "I can take you to her," he said. Then she looked down and saw the angel, Love, in a forgotten message that had wafted to Sark on the flames of the fire. She looked up with a torch raised high in the air, "I could have blessed you. I could have given you everything that you tried to steal, but because it was taken instead of given, I choose to keep it from you and until the time comes when you can graciously and unselfishly accept it, I will keep it from you!"

He felt his mother's weeping. It was something that the darkness could not offer her. There were loud cracks as the ice began to thaw, and water began to gush forth in in streams of true water as light filtered through the cracks of the black ice.

"You missed the point of the message, Mother. She does not wish to see you give into darkness, rather, she wants you to learn the true significance of the power before you can wield it. Otherwise, it is worthless."

He could see his mother now, a grey figure moving around the blackness, and her eyes blinked a deep, dark blue.

She slowly nodded her head, but then the whole castle shook. Amicus reached out to grab his mother and pulled her out of the room. She seemed heavy, and weighted, but he pulled her forward and when he reached the stone, he tapped it with his staff and suddenly he was standing in Sark.

The Astrids bowed before him and their leader, the Mother, smiled brightly as the brown stones that she wore glowed brightly.

"Welcome, son of Kialo, you've been a long time coming to us."

XXVII. The Portals

"There's someone blocking the path," said Kim, slowing the vehicle. It's not mahldrusecs, at least it doesn't look like them.

Arik sighed heavily. "They have found me," he whispered.

"Keep going," he shouted to Kim. "Don't stop. Just keep going!"

Kim stopped the vehicle anyway. "Don't stop!" he shouted again, but the ramp was already being lowered.

"They're trying to help us," said Kim, looking back at him.

Celeste, Carmina, and Arista walked inside and the ramp closed behind them. Carmina ducked and quickly sat on the floor between the seats. Arista walked to Arik as the vehicle lurched forward.

He just looked at her. Celeste stood close by, holding to the handles on the ceiling, not speaking. She was trying to take in what he had been through. Arista reached out to him.

"Arik?" she asked. Disbelief spread over her as she saw his appearance. "What happened to you?"

He was silent. Kneeling down, she reached out to his face, looking into yellow eyes that should be purple, and white hair that should be black. She ran her hands over his dark gray skin, trying to make sense of the image she saw now, so different from the brother that she had known and loved for a lifetime.

"What happened?" she asked again.

He was silent.   That question was too heavy to answer at the moment. He swallowed hard. He closed his eyes. Celeste was already affecting the mood around him.

"Just leave me alone," he pleaded.

Tears filled Arista's eyes. "No!" she exclaimed. "I will not! I will not leave you alone. Do you know how heartbroken I've been for you? How I've searched for you? The guilt I've had to deal with after what I did to you?"

He looked her then in the eyes. "Be glad you did it. The queen would have seen you wasted into nothing. I know now the extent of her power and you are better off for doing as you were told.   You could have ended up like I was …before."

"Please," she begged, "at least accept my apology."

He looked at her for a long time, then nodded.

"Arik," Celeste addressed him now. "I can never repay you for what you did for me. I didn't know what had happened to you, or I would have come for you sooner."

"I knew the risk," he said.

"Did you really?" Celeste asked. "Did you imagine the extent of her wrath?"

He shook his head. "I don't think any of us could."

Celeste nodded. A red tear traced from her eye. "We were all short-sighted. Otherwise, we would have found you first," she said. "I don't know if there's any way to fix this," she said.

"As far as I'm concerned, it has already been settled. You keep doing what you do, and don't interfere with what I intend to do. It's settled."

Celeste nodded. "I know what you're trying to do. You have no way to block me from knowing."

Arik sighed heavily. "If this is where you try to change my mind, then stop."

Celeste shook her head. "I'm not going to stop you," she said, "not after what I've learned today. In fact, I will aid you if I can."

Arik involuntarily smiled. "Well," he said, "That's something I didn't expect from you."

"I can be full of surprises," she said, "and in Sark, I'm not as naïve or as misguided as I was in Shea. I have a clear sight, and the full force of my power."

Arik nodded. "That's good. You'll need to have power. The gods are lining us up like pawns to do their will. They're using us. You, me, we're all just part of their game."

Celeste nodded. "I've known that since I was made," she said. "So, I play my part as well as I can."

"And, so will I," Arik nodded, unable to suppress his smile as he thought of the pain that he would deliver to the goddess.

Celeste soon turned away, realizing that there were so many others here that needed her. She looked at Xandra, but she didn't speak, she only pondered the strange colors that she saw. There was more pain and burden there than any of the others. She wanted to help her, but she didn't know how. She saw the pain, but she couldn't see past it to a cause, and the colors were dimmed as if she was viewing them through a veil.

Soon, the vehicle slowed, and the back door opened. Aqualon stood waiting in the sands. As the truck slowed, he walked forward, after looking at the vehicle with curiosity. Kim opened the door and he looked inside.

"I've had to close it," he said, referring to the portal. "I don't know that I want to open it again. We're all safer here. The Shadow is in Shea. I heard it," he said, holding up the shell that he had been listening to earlier. "The sea goddess told me. Things are not going so well there."

"Well, we need to get back there. We've got some wounded and the rest of our friends are there. We're not going to leave them," Kim said.

Aqualon sighed. "I might can heal your friends," he said, "before I open it again. I can't promise that you'll make it far. Some of the elves are staying to fight, but mostly, they are trying to get the other creatures to safety.

Kim nodded. "If you can heal us, then we will gladly accept your help." She motioned towards the back door.

Xandra stood and stepped out first. She didn't speak, she just began the long walk back to the city.

Shiana stepped out, calling to her, but Xandra did not respond. The others slowly filed out.

"I don't think she'll come back," said Kim, stepping out from the front. "She had her orders."

"It's too bad," said Shiana, staring after her. Arik watched her, the black filters filled his eyes again as he stepped out, making him seem shadowed, though he wasn't. He kept his arms folded. He contemplated then whether or not she even had a choice. He felt his sister beside him, her hand resting on his shoulder.

"I'll go with you," she said. He shook his head.

"No," he said, "you'll need to be here. Lead the refugees to safety."

A tense silence filled the air.

"I will not be going to Shea," said Celeste. "I'm powerless there, and I am needed here. You can lead them to me, or at least to the Scithronians. We will need their help, and we can offer them protection."

Aqualon passed them and walked over to where Michael and Sassy were still sitting by James. "Let me see him," he said. He placed a hand to his forehead and closed his eyes, searching the selbdes' mind. He stayed that way for a few moments and then he shook his head.

"I don't know that his ailment can be cured," he said.

"What's wrong with him?" Sassy asked.

"I don't know," said Aqualon. "It's strange. Magic. It's dark magic. He definitely should stay out of Shea. It is very likely that the darkness there will only progress the sickness." Celeste turned to them, and read the complicated lines in James' soul.

"I know someone that can help him," she said, "but he'll have to come with me, to the castle."

Michael shook his head. "We're not leaving him," he said. Shiana turned to them then, limping back into the vehicle.

"You don't know what he's been through," she said. "If they can heal him, we have to try. That thing on the back of his head is the only thing keeping him from killing us."

Michael shook his head. "No, we're not leaving him anywhere." Celeste knelt down to him, and took his hand in hers, looking him deep in the eyes.

"I understand why you don't want to leave him. You can come with us, if that will ease your worry. I know a great healer. She can even heal magical wounds. You have to trust that she can help him."

"I know where I've seen you before," said Michael, as a look of realization passed over his face. "I saw you, in

Shea. You came to the holding cells, but you were different then."

Celeste nodded. "I was also being held there," she said. "Please. Let me help you." Michael reluctantly nodded.

"Ok," he said, "but I'm coming too."

Aqualon turned then to Shiana. "You may need to go as well," he said. "Your leg, it's beyond my skills." Celeste looked at the wound.

"Come with us," she said. "Arista can take us close to the castle. We won't have far to walk." Teri approached them then, with Iluma in her hands.

"And what about the fairy?" she asked. "Is she even still alive?"

Aqualon looked down at the gray, shriveled thing in Teri's hands. He nodded.

"She will gain her power back in Shea. She's just spent all her magic. After rest and food, she'll gain it back.

Teri nodded. "Then I'm definitely going to Shea," she said. "We owe her a lot."

"Well, then," he said, "for those willing to enter, I will open the portal. Come close and hold hands. I will not be keeping it open this time."

Shiana turned to Sassy, "Tell David that I'm coming soon," she said. Sassy nodded.

"Of course," she said. "Take care of yourself," she said. They held a tight embrace, and then all the ones who had chosen to go to Shea held hands. Arista wrapped Arik in a hug. He just patted her back, and nodded to his sister and Celeste, and then he stepped into the circle to lock hands with the others before they vanished in a quick, blue flash.

The remaining group held hands and they vanished into a flash of white, reappearing across the island. The gates of the castle were close by. Michael carried James. Shiana leaned between Arista and Celeste for support and Carmina walked behind, her sword drawn, making sure that they did not encounter danger. After facing the creatures in the barren lands, she knew that she would have to be more vigilant. They were in Sark, and the creatures could deploy at any time.

XXVIII. King and Queen

Victor was out of the door before they could reach it. He held his arms out to Celeste, offering to take her place holding up Shiana.

"This way," he said. There was no need to ask who anyone was. He already knew each of them by reading their souls. He led them to one of the servants' bedrooms. The beds were on the bottom floor and therefore, more easily accessible. Michael laid James on the bed and Shiana sat beside him, putting her leg up. Belle was soon brought to the room by Carmina. She immediately reached out to her queen.

"I'm so glad you are back, dear," she said. Celeste nodded, and motioned to the selbdes.

"Belle, this is Michael, James, Shiana, and Arista. They too, were held in Shea. Belle, I need you to see if there is anything that you can do for them, please. We have encountered very dark magic."

Belle nodded. "I will do what I can," she said as she walked over to them. Victor put his hands in Celeste's and led her out of the room, the worry on his face increasing as they walked.

He stopped and turned to her. "I could feel something was wrong before you even got here. Tell me, Celeste. What's wrong?" She collapsed into him, holding him tightly.

"It's Darkhan," she said, swallowing back a lump of fear. "He's still here, and he's grown in power. I almost didn't get away." She stepped away and unlatched her cloak, showing him the black scorch marks, still clinging to her from the dark fire.

"Victor, anything we had questions about before...he's the answer. He's done all of it. Everything that we have suffered is because of him." Victor inhaled his anger and nodded.

"We will make it right," he said, "but first, you must take care of yourself." His concern was telling in his voice. "Don't wait until Belle heals the others. She needs to know now. We don't know how long she will take to heal them and we will need you at your strongest. Please take care of yourself."

Celeste nodded. "I will let her know," she said. She paused for a moment. "But that's not all," she added. "We found Arik," she said. Victor expected her to keep talking. He looked at her expectantly, but she just shook her head.

"What happened?" he asked.

She couldn't respond at first. "It's just too much for me to feel right now," she said. He wrapped his arms around her.

"Why didn't he come back with you?" he asked. She just cried then.

"Kristiniva. She took things from him that should never be taken. She took Luna's light from him, and she sent him to Nometheog. Vishka saved him...but he's been turned into one of those creatures from the barren lands. Now he is dedicated to the goddess of pain and suffering."

Victor sighed heavily. He remained quiet. He was trying to process everything that she was telling him. "We will find a way to set it right. All of it. I don't know how, but we will figure it out. We have to," his determination and frustration were evident as he spoke. Celeste nodded.

"We have to," she agreed. She squeezed his hand, pulling away from their embrace, and then she took out the elven cloth, using it to wipe away tears as she walked back in the room to show Belle her wounds. Victor breathed deeply. It almost came out as a growl. He would have to form a better plan. Rebuilding Sark was not what they needed. That was only part of it. They needed Nometheog, Darkhan, and Kristiniva destroyed, otherwise it would crash down faster than they could build it.

He was not supposed to kill a god. It was against their binding laws. He pondered though, where would Saigolai send them if Nometheog did not have a void? What punishment would he enact?

XXIX. The Arrivals

Victor stood by the gates, waiting. Angelik had found her way outside, and was playing in the snow. She had constructed a unique, but sturdy snow fort, and was attempting to roll up perfectly packed and round snow balls. Victor had told her why he was waiting, and she seemed to understand more than he even knew. He watched her, smiling. He helped some with the fort, remembering the days of his youth, when he had played similar games.

Back then, the castle had been a busy place, and there were plenty of other children to compete with. He was still looking at her, and in his own memories when she reached up her arm, flinging a snowball. It sailed through the air and landed with a smack as Fletcher was suddenly assaulted. Victor laughed harder than he had in a long time. Angelik laughed too, and pelted the hunter with another, which hit him so hard, that it knocked the hunter off of his feet, and he fell into the snow.

"That's enough, Angelik," Victor said, trying to suppress his laughter. He walked over and pulled the boy to his feet.

"Let's get you inside," he said. Then he looked at Angelik. "There will be more coming," he smiled at her and she smiled back as she rolled up another snow ball.

He was still laughing as he walked the hunter through the doors, taking him to Evingh. "Show him where he can clean up, and get Carmina to find him some clothes. He can eat after he's cleaned up."

Evingh looked terrified. Victor sensed it was because he was afraid that Fletcher would recognize him.

"What about these wounds?" asked Fletcher. Victor shrugged, and looked at him very seriously. "They'll heal, but not right now. I need them to stay as a reminder to you about our earlier talk."

There was a grunted response from Fletcher. Victor just looked at him. Then he turned to Evingh.

"Take him," he said. "I don't want to look at him right now." Evingh grabbed Fletcher and started to pull him out of the room.

"Get your hands off me," said Fletcher as he pulled his arm away.

"Fletcher, just go with him," said Victor. "Do what we tell you and you'll not get another burn. Defy us and you will remember your promise. This is my attendant and he must do what I ask him to. Not because he wants to, but because he must. Just like you. No go!" There was a sound of annoyance from Fletcher, but he turned then, walking with Evingh out of the room.

Celeste had entered the room, waiting for Belle to look the others over. "I don't know which spell did this," said Belle to Shiana, "but it is magical. It is dark magic. I have some things that I will try on it, but there may be a few trials before I get it right."

Shiana nodded. "If you can help, I would appreciate it."

Next Belle examined James. "What's this?" She asked, referring to the contraption on his head.

"I don't know," Shiana said, "but we can't take it off. Whatever it is, it keeps him from hurting us." Belle nodded.

"He's your healer," she said. Shiana nodded.

"How did you know?" the selbdes asked.

"I can sense it," Belle said, still looking him over in thought. "It's dark magic ailing him," she said. "Blood magic. That's the only kind that can do something like that."

"Can you help him?" Michael asked from across the room, where he leaned against the wall with his arms folded.

Belle shrugged. "I can try," she said. "I'm an earth-witch. If anyone can help him, then it is me. If I cannot help him, then no one can, 'cept Sari herself."

Belle looked at Arista then, her wounds were all flesh wounds, easily bandaged.

Arista thanked her, but stayed in the room with the others. Finally, Celeste showed Belle the dark fire, still freezing through her chest and neck.

"My queen," she said. "I'm so sorry. It's dark fire. It will be difficult to remove, but I will try." Celeste nodded.

"As the others have said, if there is anything that you can do, then it will be appreciated. I would like to be at my full-strength. I'm going to need it if Darkhan attacks us again." Belle's face turned dark and sad-looking.

"So, it's him again, is it?"

Celeste nodded. Belle sighed.

"If Slatkin were here, he would know exactly what to do."

Celeste agreed. "Maybe he will be back soon."

Belle suddenly looked old and weak. "I can't help but feel that something is wrong," she said. "He should have been back. And earlier..." she shook her head.

"What Belle?" Celeste asked.

Belle shrugged. "It was just a dream," she said. "I still get shaken by them sometimes."

Belle turned then to leave. "I'm going to go gather some items," she said. "I'll start working on some things to help you all. Until then, see if you all can rest. It sounds like you need it after what you've been through."

"See if Angelik will help you," said Celeste. "She will appreciate the work,"

"Thank you, my queen, I will ask her," she said, and then she turned to leave, looking very old and tired to Celeste.

XXX. Galan's Decision

Galan could feel the poison, still spreading through his neck. He remembered pulling the needle out, but somehow, the poison was still inside of him. He was aware of Saltook talking. There was a conversation happening with the man holding a sword, but he did not know what was being said. He felt sick, and the images of Malik, his father's death, and Haz being torn apart kept replaying in his head. He felt deaf and numb to everything around him.

Eventually, he was aware of himself falling forward, and then he dreamed...or perhaps it was real. He wasn't sure. It felt too real to be a dream. His father was there, though everything seemed dark, except for Volkhan. He was himself, fully human and alive, with no rotting flesh, wolf parts, or metal enhancements.

"Just can't get away," he said. He smoked a kial twig, and puffed out a small puff of smoke. "They'll never let me go now."

"Who?" Galan asked, confused. "Who has you?" he asked. Volkhan shook his head.

"Do you realize how many children I've fathered?"

Galan shook his head. "Some of them I know," he said. "I know there are a lot."

Volkhan nodded. "It's something to boast," he said. "And have you ever wondered why I let you stay with me? Why I chose you, out of all the others?"

Galan shrugged. "I have my mother's gift," he said. "And you knew it."

Volkhan laughed. "Something like that, but not really," he said. "That's just my excuse. That's true, but it's not the reason."

Galan shrugged. "Then I don't know," he said.

"Your mother," Volkhan started, but he couldn't seem to finish. He shook his head. There was a silence. He let out a long puff of smoke from the twig.

"What about her?" Galan asked.

"She's not at all what everyone else thinks, now is she?" he asked. "Sure, she ran. She made it hard for me sometimes. She kept her language, and her stones, and no amount of beating could take it away from her, but it was a show," he said, puffing out more smoke. The room started to fill with it.

"Your mother enjoyed power as much as anyone else. Every time I gave her a prized fur, or brought her with me on a hunt, I could see it in her eyes." He gazed off into the distance, as if re-living a memory that was only known to him.

"She enjoyed it. She loved being in that position. Put on a pedestal. She was respected because of it. No other man would touch her, because they all knew that I would have killed them...if she didn't beat me to it. She was royalty in this tribe, she would have had a crown of antlers if she would have been born to a hunter, and she could have gotten away if she really wanted to. Hell, she was faster than I was. This leg, it's not felt the same since it broke, until...well there were some benefits to my change." He waved the thought away.

"So, you loved her then?" Galan asked.

Volkhan shrugged. "If that's what it is called," he said. "I enjoyed the chase, and she enjoyed giving me something to chase, but that's not the point, son. That's just what you're gathering from it."

Galan looked at his father in confusion. "So, what are you trying to tell me?"

Volkhan breathed deeply. "You're the only one that felt like a real son," he said. "I gave you gifts that I didn't give the others. I taught you things that I never cared to show the others."

"But why?" Galan asked.

Volkhan shrugged. "Because you were like your mother. The other women, the mothers of the other children, they wanted what she had, but they couldn't carry it the way that she could...and the other children, most of them either don't know that I'm their father, or they envy you, but that envy could turn into something else. It could be submission when they see what you can do. You could be a leader. But even if you lead, some of them will always desire your position and your woman, whoever you choose. Consider this a warning. Watch your back, son. They'll look you in the eye and stab you in the heart."

"Kaila wouldn't," he said. Volkhan shook his head, smiling at the thought. "No, she wouldn't, but there are others who would." His face turned serious again.

"Son, I've done some things that I regret. My first son, you've known him. Darkhan. He was around for a while when you were younger. His mother was Quinlan, and he was the only other gifted son I ever had, that I know of. His mother died giving birth to him, so he never knew her. I tried to teach him, but he was spoiled with a darkness from his youth. I was still a boy then, really. I was still making sense of the world. The thought of having to be a father was terrifying enough...I did the best I could. It's hard to keep a child alive without their mother, but I did it...for a while anyway. The things that he did, from so young of an age scared me more than being a father...I don't even like to think of it. He enjoyed the killing, but not just the killing. It was the pain, and the torture...and even as a young boy, he could do cruel things that I had never thought to imagine. I should have killed him, but I didn't. I left him with an old woman in the woods. She offered me riches and said that she would look after him. I was unaware that she was a scout for the temple of Nometheog. She raised him for a while, and when she learned how gifted he was, she presented him to the temple. Truth be told, I was glad to be rid of the burden, but I regret it now. She saw something that I had overlooked. He was raised in the temple of Nometheog, and later, came back to find me, after he was already a priest.

For a while, he was there, holding power over me, trying to bend me to his will, competing for dominance of the tribe. I did as he asked, trying to make up for those mistakes. But there's really no coming back from what I did to him. He left one day. I hoped for good. He destroyed the temple many years ago. The woman that cared for him is long dead with all the priests of the temple. I often wondered where he went with no place to call home. I figured he was dead, too, but he's still here."

Volkhan put a hand on Galan's shoulder. "He means you great harm, but I know that you are the only one that stands a chance of stopping him. I kept you close because I was hoping that you would save us if he ever found me again." There was silence.

"Of course, I was wrong. He found me anyway, through the deception of the arms dealer and now here we are."

"So, is he the one that changed you?" Galan asked. Volkhan nodded his head.

"Yes, and no. He had a part in it, but so did the arms dealer. They did it together. I may seem dead, but I'm not. Darkhan controls my soul. I can't live and I can't die."

"Do you want to live or die?" asked Galan.

Volkhan shrugged. "Either of them would be better than this," he said. "What happened between us earlier...forget it. That wasn't me. That's all him. I might give you a stern beating, but I would never..." he stopped talking then, and turned with his back to Galan and pulled up his hood. "Now, go on," he said. "You're the only one that can help me."

Galan nodded. "I will help you, if I can," he said, "but how do I do that? Will I have to kill you again?"

Volkhan shrugged. "Maybe, but that's not what it is at all. We will see when the time comes. Just know this, he wants you. He'll try to use me to hunt you down. I'll find you, and when I do, you'll know what to do. Just pray I track you down before he does. If he finds you, then I'll never be free, and neither will you." Suddenly his father was pulled away and the darkness was all encompassing.

Galan opened his eyes, fully awake and sitting up, his heart racing with fear. He was in one of the huts by the river. Saltook was sitting outside the door, smoking a pipe. further away, he could see a group of people gathered by a fire. He wiped away a cold sweat, as he tried to fight back the tears of panic and shaking that his dream had brought. He looked around for his pack. It was on the table beside of him. He stopped for a moment. His heart was frozen in his chest.

A kial twig was on the table, still lit, a trail of thin smoke curled up from it. He reached out, shaking in fear to feel it. It was as real as anything else in the room. He put it out, then grabbed his pack, placing the half-smoked twig inside, before placing the pack over his shoulder. He still felt weak and fevered, but he knew that he had to go. Saltook turned to him.

"You're already awake?" he asked. Galan nodded.

317

"I have to go," he said. Saltook nodded.

"They're cooking fish for us," he said. "They need to talk to you."

"Me?" he asked. "Why? What do they want to know?"

"They need to tell you something, and I think they have some questions," he said.

Galan sighed. "I don't have time to answer questions. I need to go."

"We will leave tomorrow, when it is warmer, and when you are feeling better."

"My father," said Galan, "I don't think he's dead," he said. "I think he's coming back for me."

"Galan, you stabbed him with holy kial fire. There is no way that he can come back from that."

"There's a way," said Galan, stubbornly.

"Do it for me," said Saltook. "These people healed that poison in you. You owe them," he said.

"Fine," said Galan, "but I'm leaving in the morning whether we're done talking or not. We've already wasted too much time talking."

"Come on," said Saltook. "Come talk to them now." Galan sighed deeply, then nodded and followed Saltook, wishing that he could already be across the island.

XXXI. Dark Immortals

Vishka closed her eyes, smiling at the secrets that she held, secrets that no one could take from her, even as she felt the squeeze of Nometheog's chains raking into her skin and burning against her flesh. She could not see anything physically in the blackest cavern, void of light, memory, and life. The chains rolled against her, holding her tighter than before, so that she could not move. She savored the burn. Nometheog struck her then, and she smiled. A mix of excitement, hidden secrets, and all-knowledge filled her until she could only laugh. It came out as a deep growl that shook the cavern.

"You will not escape again," he said to her.

She laughed again, as she saw with far-sight. She could see him, her creation, moving towards his goal.

"Your challenges...your abuse...they give me a reasoning and thought," she said. "Hit me again!" she ordered. Nometheog refused.

"You will forget it all," he said, "in time." She smiled then. The void of darkness gave her clarity of vision, clarity of what her secrets could tell. She might forget, but there was now a creature that never would, one bound to her. One that would never chain away her gifts.

Darkhan lay in his meditation and healing until he could no longer remember what had caused his pain. The void consumed him yet again, and his dark vitality returned. He stood and walked until he found himself lingering over the dead hunter, Volkhan.

Shekley stood with him. He did not remember being summoned by him, but here he was.

"We can't rebuild what was burned by the fire," Shekley said, examining the body. His eyes were black and he seemed more humored than he had been for days. "Thiera stands against us, but I had her cast out before. I will do it again." His voice was high-pitched.

"Kristiniva has lost the angel," Shekley said. Darkhan could feel the frustration from the Shadow. "I understand you fought with her."

"I did," he said. "She is stronger now. That's why we had to strike when we did. Now, I don't know that I can fight her alone," said Darkhan. "I will have to find a way to weaken her."

"We will find the solution," said Shekley. "David, Shiana, the angels, and the boy. All are vital. We need the boy and the selbdes alive. The angels, we must destroy."

"But how?" asked Darkhan.

"The boy is the key," he said. "For now, let us send his father back to him."

Darkhan nodded, and fumbled for something in his robes. It was a necklace with a wolf tooth amulet. "I will summon him at your word," he said. Shekley nodded.

"You will do that and more. I will make him a new body. This one has been corrupted by Thiera," he said. He turned away from the body and walked over to his rows of machinery and metal.

"I need him to find the boy."

"He's the only one that can find him," said Darkhan. "I have tried, but he evades all of my magic."

The Shadow nodded Shekley's head. "We must find him before the other gods can see our intent. We will work quickly. Come, I need your assistance."

Darkhan was suddenly across the room, watching in interest as Shekley began to assemble the parts that would soon house Volkhan's soul.

www.ingramcontent.com/pod-product-compliance
Lightning Source LLC
Chambersburg PA
CBHW020908200626
46814CB00001BA/231